W9-ATK-044

THE CHANGELINGS

CHRISTINA SOONTORNVAT

sourcebooks
jabberwocky

Published by Sourcebooks Jabberwocky, an imprint of Sourcebooks, Inc.
P.O. Box 4410, Naperville, Illinois 60567-4410
(630) 961-3900
Fax: (630) 961-2168
www.sourcebooks.com

Library of Congress Cataloging-in-Publication Data

Names: Soontornvat, Christina, author.
Title: The Changelings / Christina Soontornvat.
Description: Naperville, Illinois : Sourcebooks Jabberwocky, [2016] |

  Summary: When eleven-year-old Izzy's sister, Hen, disappears into the
  woods near their new house, Izzy, aided by a band of outlaw Changelings,
  must seek her in the land of Faerie.
Identifiers: LCCN 2015039331 | (alk. paper)
Subjects: | CYAC: Missing children--Fiction. | Shapeshifting--Fiction. |
  Magic--Fiction. | Sisters--Fiction. | Fantasy.

Classification: LCC PZ7.1.S677 Ch 2016 | DDC [Fic]--dc23 LC record available at https://lccn.loc.gov/2015039331

Source of Production: Worzalla, Stevens Point, Wisconsin, USA
Date of Production: July 2016
Run Number: 5007037

Printed and bound in the United States of America.
WOZ 10 9 8 7 6 5 4 3 2 1

for
Iliana and Verena

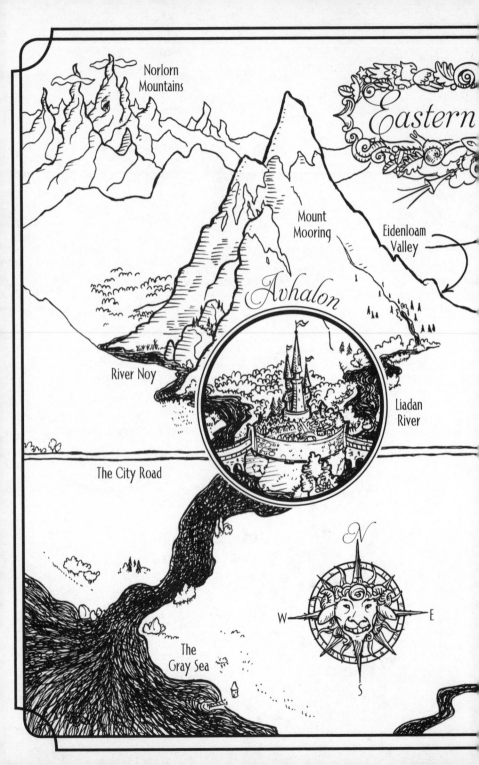

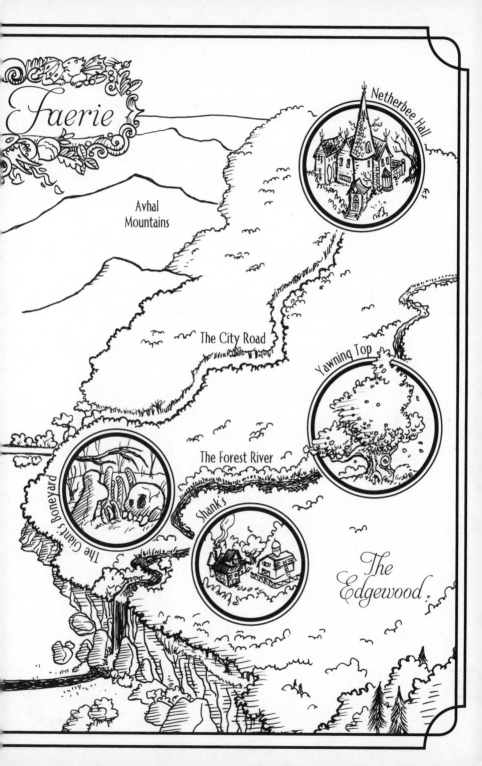

Wee Bretabairn, born in the caul,
Child of none, mime of all.
With dimpled cheeks and fine, white teeth,
Mother won't guess what hides beneath.
Father, too, will never know
His babe's a fey in man-child clothes.

from The Bretabairn,
a fairy book of poems

OVERHEARD AT THE JIGGLY GOAT

Izzy Doyle stood in the school supply section of the Jiggly Goat, coming to terms with her fate. She'd agreed to go with her mom and sister to the grocery store because she needed a new journal. As she faced her only options—yellow legal pad or inspirational kittens—the full weight of her situation came crashing down on her narrow shoulders.

This was it. Her new hometown.

Her little sister bounded down the aisle, blond curls swishing behind her. "Guess what? They don't have that gross healthy cereal Mom likes, so she's letting us get Kookoo Crunchies!"

"That's awesome," said Izzy. Hen could be happy living on the surface of the moon as long as there were snacks.

Izzy turned her back on the measly journal offerings and trudged after her sister toward the checkout counter. She still couldn't believe it. During the eleven years she'd been alive, her family had lived in nine different cities, and her parents had to choose this one to settle down in. Everton didn't even count as a city. Cities had museums and libraries. Everton had a grocery store named after a wiggling farm animal.

We're getting back to our roots, her parents had said. *Fresh air*, they'd said. *Nature*. Izzy hadn't connected the dots until now. When they said "nature," what they really meant was complete isolation from the rest of civilization.

Izzy's mom stood at the counter, chatting with the cashier. He wore a blue apron with a smiling goat on the front and a package of beef jerky sticking out of the pocket.

"I'm telling you," he said as he scanned the groceries. "That neighbor of yours is a witch, or I'm a bull toad."

Witch.

The hairs on Izzy's forearms stood up. She squeezed past the shopping cart to get closer.

Her mom smiled politely and took out her wallet. "I beg your pardon?"

The cashier narrowed his eyes and ran his tongue across a silver tooth. "You wanna know what she came in here and bought last week?"

"I can't ima—"

"*Beef tongue.* Now I ask you, what kind of person buys that? Puts it in a potion or something, I bet."

Izzy's mom started lifting the sacks into the cart. "I'm afraid we haven't had the pleasure of meeting Mrs. Malloy yet."

"Oh, it ain't *Mrs.* You think anyone would marry her?

2

Shoot, no. Marian Malloy would sooner put a curse on a man than say hello." The cashier leaned his elbow against the register. "If it were me that inherited that big house of yours, I'd sell it to the first fool who'd buy it from me."

Izzy slid over to where Hen stood eyeing a display of Moon Pies. "Ask Mom to take you to the bathroom," she whispered.

"But I don't have to go," Hen said.

"I know that! It's just a diversion."

"A what?"

"Ugh, forget it!"

Izzy tried to think of some other way to distract her mom so she could keep the cashier talking about the witch. Before she could come up with anything, their mom finished paying and herded them out of the store to the parking lot.

Their mom laughed as she unlocked the back hatch of the car. "Country people are so superstitious! Your dad is going to get a real kick out of it when I tell him we have to sell his mother's house because a 'witch' lives next door."

Izzy stood next to the car, drumming her fingers on the door handle. Having a witch for a neighbor would mean they actually hadn't moved to the most boring place on Earth. She peered through the window into the back of the car. From the amount of groceries they bought, she could tell they wouldn't be coming back for at least a week. If she wanted to hear any more about the witch, this was her best chance.

Izzy started to jog back across the parking lot. "Hey, Mom, I think I left something in there…"

"What? Sweetie, what did you leave?"

"Oh gosh, I left my favorite book! I'll be right back!"

The sliding doors whooshed open, and Izzy hurried to the cash register. The cashier's face was hidden behind a cheap tabloid newspaper. The cover read, *Aliens spotted at Tullahoma Waffle House.*

Izzy tapped on the counter. "Excuse me?"

"Whatcha need, sugar?" he replied without putting his paper down.

"Was everything you said really true? About our neighbor being a witch, I mean."

The cashier crumpled the tabloid and leaned toward her. "Oh, it's the truth, all right. And you little girls need to watch yourselves out there."

"Why? What could happen to us?"

The cashier's voice dropped to a whisper, and his eyes scanned side to side. "Folks seen her roamin' them woods around her house, even at night. Anyone tries to go near there, she runs 'em off. She says she's watchin' out for the *fairies*, but I'll bet you she's hidin' somethin'. Like a big pile of human bones."

The front doors of the store slid open. "Izzy, your book's in the car," said her mom. "Come on. We need to get home to let Dublin out."

Izzy reluctantly turned and followed after her. She stole one last look at the cashier. He was back to his tabloid, gnawing at a piece of beef jerky on a string. Izzy sighed. Not exactly the most reliable source of information. Still, if a witch wanted to hide away from civilized society, Everton was definitely the place. Fingers crossed, Izzy got into the car, and her mom started the long, pothole-riddled drive out to their new, old house.

A NEIGHBORLY VISIT

IZZY TRIED TO IGNORE the drops of sweat rolling down the bridge of her nose, but her little sister was making it difficult.

"It's so hot it's compressive," whined Hen.

"You mean *oppressive*." Izzy wiped her forehead on her sleeve. Even though it was technically the first day of fall, summer still held Everton tight in its sticky grip. "If you're going to complain, then just go back home."

Izzy knew that would silence the whining for at least a few minutes. She and Hen sat huddled behind an azalea bush at the end of the long gravel driveway leading up to Marian Malloy's house. They'd been waiting for a glimpse of the old woman for almost an hour. If she didn't come out soon, they'd have to go home for dinner with nothing to show for their patience.

Hen picked up an acorn and chucked it into the drainage ditch beside them. "If you want to see her so bad, why don't you just go knock on the door?"

"Are you crazy? You don't just go knocking on a witch's front door!"

"Mom says she's not a witch," said Hen. "She says we should be nice to her, because she's just a lonely old lady."

"So was the woman in the gingerbread house, but that didn't stop her from trying to eat Hansel and Gretel, did it?"

"Dad says she was friends with Grandma Jean."

"That's even more reason to be suspicious of her!"

Izzy and Hen had never met their father's mother. After Izzy was born, Grandma Jean had turned into a complete recluse, refusing their visits and never answering their letters. She didn't even leave them the Everton house in her will. If Izzy's dad hadn't hired a lawyer, the musty old house would have gone to the state, and Izzy would still have her own room instead of having to share one with a seven-year-old.

Izzy rolled up her T-shirt sleeves. "Hand me Dad's binoculars," she whispered. "Maybe I can see something through the windows."

Hen slipped off her sparkly purple backpack and started rummaging around inside.

"Shhh! You're making too much noise!" Izzy reached over and took the backpack. Inside, her fingers ran over strands of costume jewelry and a jumble of plastic toys. "Wait a second—what's this?" She pulled out a handful of small paper cones with short strings coming out the top.

Hen scratched the side of her freckled nose, the way she

always did when she was lying. "Huh, now how did those get in there?"

"Hen! You know you're not allowed to have fireworks!" Izzy tossed the cones into the ditch. Hen had an obsession with all things combustible, and this wasn't the first time Izzy had caught her with a secret stash. "Do you want to blow us both up or something?"

"Crackle Caps can't blow anything up," said Hen sadly. "I thought we could use them to create a *diversion*. You know, for the witch."

"We have to spot her first," said Izzy. She held the binoculars up to her eyes and peered around the bush.

Marian's house was nestled far back from the road, close to the dense tangle of woods that separated the old woman's property from theirs. Rows of fat, golden corn and vibrant vegetables surrounded the house, filling up most of the large yard. Brown-and-white goats bleated softly from their pen behind the house. Everything else was quiet.

Izzy hoped they hadn't started out too late. Today was the perfect day to spy. Their dad had driven to Nashville to do research for his new book, and their mom had shooed them out of the house so she could paint the living room. Who knew when they'd get such a good chance again?

From the side of the farmhouse, Izzy heard the creak of a rusty hinge. She swiveled the binoculars in time to see the garden shed door swing open. An old woman emerged, carrying a bucket in one hand and a spade in the other.

"She doesn't really look like a witch to me," said Hen.

"You can't tell anything about her just by looking," whispered Izzy, but she had to admit that Hen was right.

Izzy had hoped for an ancient crone or an icy sorceress—the kind of witches she'd read about in *Faerie and Folktales of Yesteryear*. But the tall woman tromping into her garden looked more like a farmer than anything else. Her pants were tucked into mud-stained boots, and her rolled-up sleeves revealed splotchy, tanned arms. Despite her wrinkles, she looked strong and didn't stoop the way most old people did.

The woman plopped the bucket down beside one of the vegetable beds and started sprinkling a red powder over the lush plants.

"Can I see?" whispered Hen at Izzy's shoulder.

"There's nothing to see yet," said Izzy. "She's just gardening. Wait a second—now she's standing up again."

Marian Malloy marched to the edge of her garden, where the trees of the surrounding woods cast her vegetable beds into deep shade. Izzy thumbed the dial until the old woman snapped into focus again. She stood facing the woods with one hand resting on a tree trunk. She lifted up her crumpled hat and passed a hand through her short, white hair. Eyes shut, she took in several slow breaths. It seemed to Izzy like she was listening, waiting for something.

The old woman opened her eyes. She frowned and shook her head, then bent down to tend to something at the base of the tree. Izzy stretched up a little taller, angling the binoculars down at the thing at the old woman's feet. It looked like a short stack of stones. Izzy swept the binoculars over the rest of the yard. More of the strange stacks of rocks stood at regular intervals all along the perimeter of the old woman's property.

"That's so weird!" she whispered to Hen.

"Can I see? What is it?"

Izzy lowered the binoculars and held them against her chest. "She's got all these funny little stone towers around her yard."

"What, like that one?"

Hen pointed to the old woman's mailbox, just a few feet away from them. A stack of stones lay nestled in the long grass at its base.

"Exactly like that one."

Before Izzy could say anything, Hen scooted over to the stones and picked the top one off the stack.

"Careful! They could be laced with poison or something like that," said Izzy. She shuffled closer and leaned forward, peering over her sister's shoulder.

Underneath the rock lay a single oak leaf, pressed flat, its edges still fresh and green. Hen lifted up the next rock, then the next. A different species of leaf lay sandwiched between each stone, five in all. The back of Izzy's neck tingled. If this wasn't witch behavior, then nothing was.

"What do you think it is?" whispered Hen.

"Could be anything. Maybe some kind of trap to lure little children to her house. Or a signal so other witches know what she is." Izzy raised the binoculars again to watch the old woman. "Maybe we can catch her saying an incantation or something like that."

Hen reached up for the binoculars. "I want to see. It's my turn to look."

"Not yet."

"You've had them forever already!" Hen lunged for them and slipped, crunching her tennis shoes into the gravel.

Izzy winced and glanced back up at Marian Malloy, who stood up quickly and darted her eyes around the yard like a wary bird. Izzy held her breath. The old woman brushed her dirty hands against her legs and turned to go inside her house. Izzy exhaled with relief.

She glared at Hen. *Be quiet*, she mouthed, reluctantly passing her the binoculars.

Hen peered through them at the house. Her tongue flicked the space where her top two teeth used to be. "She's in the kitchen," she whispered.

"What's she doing?" asked Izzy. "Crushing herbs? Mixing a potion?"

"She's...she's...washing dishes."

"Is that all?"

"OK, wait, now she's doing something else. She moved

away from the window." Hen scanned the binoculars side to side. "I think she went into a different room or something…"

Izzy frowned and squinted at the house. Now that she'd seen the stone towers, she wanted to catch the old woman doing something even witchier. Hadn't the Jiggly Goat cashier said something about a pile of bones? That would be perfect.

Izzy heard the unmistakable sound of wet, fast breathing a moment before something warm and heavy bowled her over.

"Dublin!" said Hen, opening her arms to let their black Labrador lick her face.

Izzy grabbed the dog by his collar and pulled him down beside her. "Sit, Dublin, sit! Hen, what is he doing here? I thought I told you to lock him inside!"

"I did!"

"You obviously didn't! He's going to give us away."

A gruff voice above them said, "You gave yourselves away long before he showed up."

LEAF AND STONE

IZZY FELT HER STOMACH jump right up into her eyeballs.
She whirled around to see the old woman towering over
them, a deep scowl etched into her face. Hen screamed and
let the binoculars clatter to the ground. Izzy lunged backward,
knocking over the stack of stones next to the mailbox.

"I've been waiting for you girls to come around," said the
woman, taking a slow step toward them. "Come here and let
Old Malloy get a look at you."

Hen sprung up off the asphalt like a click beetle and took
off running down the road. Izzy scrambled to her feet, somehow managing to scoop up the binoculars and backpack at the
same time. She flew down the pavement after her sister, her
legs whirring beneath her, hair whipping her face.

The old woman's voice rang out after them. "Wait! You
girls come back here!"

Dublin rocketed past them, a black blur on the tar road.

Izzy didn't dare turn around. She pumped her legs at high speed as they ran down the hill, past the woods, and up their gravel driveway. Even then, she didn't stop until they were safely back in their kitchen with the door shut behind them.

"That was…the scaredest…I've ever been…in my life!" said Hen, panting and laughing at the same time.

Izzy leaned against the pantry door, clutching her stomach. Once she caught her breath, she grabbed *Faerie and Folktales of Yesteryear* off the kitchen island and took it to the table.

Hen leaned in beside her. "What are you doing?"

"I want to see if I can find anything written about those stone towers," said Izzy, flipping to the index. "I wonder if they're some kind of magic talisman or a charm or something like that."

"Wow, yeah, I bet they are," said Hen, bouncing on her toes. "This is so awesome. Izzy, isn't it awesome?"

"Isn't what awesome?" asked their mom as she walked into the kitchen. On the stove, a pot clanked and burbled, and the room filled with a stewed, green smell. "And why did you lock Dublin inside? The poor guy was crying like a baby until I let him out."

"I *told* you!" said Hen, sticking out her tongue. "It's Mom's fault we got caught by the witch, not mine."

"Witch?" Izzy's mom spun around from the stove. "Isabella Doyle, have you been bothering that poor old woman after I specifically told you not to?"

Izzy glared at Hen. She shut her book and stood up to face her mom. "We weren't bothering her. We were just watching her. She wouldn't even have known we were there if Hen hadn't made so much noise."

"Well, you shouldn't hog things all to yourself," said Hen.

Their mom began pulling dinner plates out of the cabinet. "She probably thinks we're the worst neighbors in the world. I'll have to take her a zucchini loaf as a peace offering." She filled up the drink glasses and handed them to Hen. "You two are not allowed to go over there again unless you're with me, all right?"

Izzy helped lay out the place settings. Why couldn't Hen ever keep her big mouth shut? Marian Malloy was the one interesting thing Everton had going for it, and now they'd never be able to spy on her again.

"I knew I should have gone by myself," she grumbled.

"You always want to leave me behind," Hen whined as she carried the glasses to the table. "You're not the only one who wants to have an adventure, you know! You don't have to be so—oops…"

Izzy looked up in time to see a full glass of lemonade tumble out of Hen's hands and right onto *Faerie and Folktales of Yesteryear.*

"Hen! *What* did you do?"

"It's OK, just need to soak it up a little…" Hen opened the cover of the book and dabbed at the sticky pages with a wad of paper napkins.

"Stop it! You're making it worse!" Izzy dropped the silver-ware. She grabbed the book out of Hen's hands, and a soggy page ripped away.

"Don't look at me," said Hen. "That was your fault."

"It's *your* fault for being so clumsy!" shouted Izzy. "And just stop touching it! You're not allowed to come near this book anymore."

Hen's lower lip began to quiver. "But—but you said you'd read me Sir Gawain and the Jolly Green Giant."

Izzy held the wet page against her chest, trying to dry it off. It stuck to her shirt and ripped in half. "Ugh, you always ruin everything! I wish I'd left you behind and let the witch eat you!"

"Girls, that's enough!" said their mom, slamming the butter dish onto the table. "If you two are going to argue, then you need to take it in the other room."

Hen shoved her way past Izzy and stomped up the stairs, snot dribbling out her nose. She shut their bedroom door so hard that it shook the pictures on the walls.

Their mom looked up at the ceiling. When she turned to Izzy, her voice was full of disappointment and anger all mixed together. "Isabella Doyle, what in the world has gotten into you? You need to go and apologize to your sister!"

"Me? What about what she just did?"

"It was an accident. Besides, it's just a book. You take those stories of yours way too seriously."

"You always take her side."

"That's not true," said her mom. She walked over to Izzy and placed her hands on her shoulders. "Listen. You know how much Hen looks up to you. It's not easy moving to a new place, and she needs her big sister right now. And you need her too."

Izzy rolled her eyes. She needed Hen like she needed appendicitis. "If it's all so hard on her, then why did we move in the first place? I never wanted to live in this town."

"This house is very special. You know that. Your dad was born here. And you were too, let's not forget." The phone rang. "That's probably your dad," said her mom with a sigh. "Izzy, this move is a chance for all of us to make a fresh start, you included. But that means you'll have to stop hiding behind your books all the time. OK, sweetie?"

Izzy groaned and tramped onto the side porch. The screen door slapped behind her as she flung herself into a chair. The sun had just set, and already the insects thrummed their nightly chant. She sat there a while, plucking the wicker out of the armrest.

A fresh start. What a joke. Monday would be Izzy's *tenth* fresh start at a new school, and she had no reason to expect things would go any better than they had before. Her sister, on the other hand, would make a whole flock of new friends by the time the bell rang. Fitting in was written into Hen's DNA. Somehow that gene had skipped over Izzy.

She twisted a fraying piece of wicker until it snapped off.

It didn't matter. She didn't need friends. She for sure didn't need her baby sister hanging around her heels. All she needed was *Faerie and Folktales of Yesteryear*. But now the book that she'd carried with her to every new hometown lay in a sticky, ruined heap on the kitchen table.

Dublin let himself out onto the porch and nosed his head into Izzy's lap. She rubbed him under the ears.

"You know they're more than just stories, don't you, Dub? Of course you do. You're on my side."

At least someone was. Right now, Izzy wished it were all reversed—that the stories were real, and this life was just a nice little fable she could close the cover on whenever her family drove her crazy.

Dublin suddenly swung his head away from her lap. He skittered to the edge of the porch, barking loudly at the front yard. He must have smelled a rabbit or a skunk. Their city dog had no idea what to do with himself now that he was surrounded by wildlife.

"Go on, Dub. Go catch it," said Izzy.

But the dog wouldn't leave the porch. He just kept yelping and looking over his shoulder at her.

"Izzy!" called her mom from inside the house. "Get him to settle down! I'm trying to talk to your dad."

"Dub, you are such a fraidycat," said Izzy, getting up from her chair. "Come on!"

She jumped down off the porch onto the grass, with Dublin

following behind. In the failing light, she saw something cross the yard and head for the trees on the edge of their property. Something much bigger than a rabbit.

Izzy hung back within running distance of her house while Dublin bolted out into the middle of the yard, barking at the darkness in all directions.

"Dublin, be quiet!"

As Izzy scanned the shadows, she saw a dark shape cross the bottom of their driveway. She took a step forward, but before she could get a good look, the shape disappeared into the blackness of the road. It moved so fast, she couldn't tell what it was. A deer, maybe? Dublin had stopped barking and walked in tight circles, sniffing the grass.

"Come on, boy. Let's go inside," said Izzy.

But Dublin wouldn't come. He stood snuffling at a spot in the middle of the yard. She didn't want to leave him outside in case the shadow she saw was another dog. Dublin would get destroyed in a dogfight. She walked to him and grabbed his collar.

"I said come on, Dub."

But before she could yank him toward the house, something on the ground caught her eye. She bent down and pulled the blades of grass apart with her fingers. It was a tower of five flat stones. Izzy picked the top stone off the stack. A single fresh leaf lay beneath it. Izzy's neck prickled again. This was just like the towers she'd seen at Marian Malloy's house.

That shadow she'd seen was no animal. Was their neighbor trying to put a curse on them for spying on her?

Izzy looked back down at the road just as the lights of her dad's car turned into the driveway. She held on to Dublin while her dad rumbled up the gravel drive and parked beside the house. Her first thought was to run up to him and tell him all about the stone towers and the shadowy figure she saw. But then she remembered what her mom had said. They would probably tell her she was just imagining things, that she'd been reading too many fairy tales.

They wanted her to be normal, to get her nose out of her books. Maybe it was time to give them what they wanted.

"There's my girl," said her dad as he shut the car door and walked toward her. He took a deep breath and let it out with a smile. "You and Dub must be out here listening to the sweet sounds of peace and relaxation." His beard prickled her forehead when he bent down and kissed her. "What's for dinner?"

"Broccoli surprise, I think."

"Eesh." Her dad made a face, then winked at her. "Hey, sweetie, is everything all right? You look like something's on your mind."

With a flick of her toe, Izzy scattered the tower of stones. "Nope. Everything's perfectly normal."

Then she followed her dad into the house with Dublin at her heels.

COME AWAY,
O HUMAN CHILD

THE NEXT MORNING WAS Sunday. Izzy lay in bed with the blanket pulled up over her face, expecting Hen to pounce on her any minute, just like she did every day. When it still hadn't happened, she yanked the covers down and sat up. Hen's bed was an empty, rumpled mess of sheets and stuffed animals. Izzy sat for a minute, listening for the sound of her sister belting out Christmas carols even though it was three months too early. But the house was quiet. At her feet, Dublin rolled lazily onto his side.

Izzy slid out of bed. She found a pair of jeans and a T-shirt in one of the moving boxes labeled *School Clothes*. The thought of walking through the doors of yet another new school the next morning nearly made her crawl back into bed.

Dublin rubbed up beside her. "You're right, Dub. Not like we haven't done it before. Come on. Let's get you some food."

At the mention of food, Dublin raced ahead of her down the stairs. On their way to the kitchen, they met her mom in the front hall, carrying two cans of paint.

"There you are." She leaned over and planted a kiss on Izzy's cheek. "I was just about to come wake you up."

"What time is it?" asked Izzy.

"Eight thirty. There's toast and orange juice still on the table if you're hungry."

Izzy scooped out food for Dublin, then sat down at the table. "Hey, Mom? Where's Hen?"

"She's playing outside, sweetie," her mom called from the living room. "When you're done eating, can you go out and keep an eye on her? She said she packed some food for you to have a picnic later."

Izzy looked down at the end of the table where *Faerie and Folktales* lay open, all the pages now permanently wrinkled. She slid another piece of blackened toast onto her plate. Her sister could wait.

As she choked down the burnt toast, Izzy looked around the dining room, still decorated with her dead grandmother's knickknacks. A collection of porcelain owls lined the shelves, and strands of tiny silver bells crisscrossed every window. Izzy couldn't believe she was actually born here. Her parents had been on a surprise visit to her grandmother when her mom went into labor a month early. From what she knew of her birth story, it was a pretty nerve-racking night. But everything had turned out OK, aside from Izzy always being small for her age. That was the first and last time she had set foot in the house until they moved to Everton.

After Izzy filled in the crossword her dad had left unfinished, she went to the back door and slipped on her high-tops while Dublin bounced around her with his tongue hanging out.

"Yes, yes, you can come this time," said Izzy.

"Take a sweater!" called her mom.

Izzy cracked the door. It had to be almost ninety degrees out, but she yanked her sweatshirt off the coat rack anyway, tied it around her waist, and headed outside. She strolled out through the open field behind the house, heading for the boulder pile on the edge of their property and the forest. A cool breeze cut through the humid air and blew a scattering of yellow-tipped leaves across the grass. Izzy heard a *pop, pop, pop*, and then Hen's mess of golden curls appeared over the top of the boulders. Izzy couldn't help smiling. Her sister must have squirreled away a serious stash of Crackle Caps.

Izzy raised her hand to get Hen's attention but stopped in midwave.

She heard music.

She cupped her ears and pointed them back at her house. But this didn't sound like her mom's usual Broadway soundtracks. It was a flute. The song was sweet, a little sad, and familiar somehow, though Izzy couldn't think where she would have heard it before. She turned back to the boulders, where Hen scratched at the rocks with a stick, nodding her head to the same tune.

Izzy started walking toward her sister again. "Hey, Hen! Mom said you wanted to play." For some reason, the words came out sounding shaky.

Hen didn't look up. Instead, she turned around and faced the trees, clapping her hands to the music. Izzy looked down at Dublin, but he just panted along beside her, as happy as she'd ever seen him. Izzy told herself she was being silly, but she started walking faster anyway. A thick feeling had crept into the back of her throat, the same feeling she had when she knew something terrible was about to happen on the next page of a story.

"Hen? Hey, come here for a second."

Hen continued staring into the trees like someone who'd been hypnotized. Then she scrambled over the top of the boulders and disappeared down the other side.

Izzy swallowed, but the thick feeling in her throat wouldn't go away. She jogged straight for the boulder pile, with Dublin close behind.

"Hen, I'm not mad at you, OK? I'm ready to play with you now!"

The music grew louder—it was definitely not coming from the house. It drifted toward them from *inside* the woods. Izzy scanned the undergrowth for the source of the notes but didn't see anyone.

As she rounded the boulders, she called again, "Hen, come here! Please!"

With a lurch in her stomach, Izzy watched as Hen skipped right into the forest.

"Stop! *Wait!*"

Izzy sprinted to the tree line. A sudden breeze blew out of the woods onto her face. With the next train of notes from the flute, the heady smell of flowers filled her nostrils. She pressed the heels of her hands into her eyes. What was happening?

Dublin sat at her feet, no hackles raised, his ears not even perked up. He lay down and set his head on his paws. Izzy grabbed his collar and pulled him toward the woods.

"Come on, you lazy dog!"

Dublin grunted and closed his eyes. Izzy wrenched on his collar as hard as she could, but he wouldn't budge. She let go of him and plunged into the woods, crashing through the brambles. She ran to the spot where she last saw her sister, but she couldn't find her. She swung her head back and forth, searching the forest. Finally, she spotted Hen zipping through the trees, following after the receding notes of the flute. How could she already be so far away?

Izzy lifted her feet high so she wouldn't trip on the stones jutting out of the ground. Thorny vines caught at her sweatshirt and clawed her ankles and hands. The harder she pushed ahead, the more they pulled her back. All the while, the familiar music played on in the distance.

"Hey, wait for me!"

She fumbled frantically to yank herself free from the thorns. Hen was now far away, a tiny dot of red between the trees.

"Hen, you stop *right now!*" She tried to sound authoritative, but she could hear the fear in her voice.

Izzy ran. The tangled undergrowth blocked her way like razor wire as she darted one way and then the other. No matter how hard she tried, she couldn't close the distance between herself and the little fleck of red flitting deeper and deeper into the woods. Gasping for breath, she stopped and leaned over with her hands on her knees.

"Hen? Hen!"

The speck of red was gone. She had lost her.

Panic bubbled up inside her chest. Izzy turned around, searching for the way she came, but the trees looked the same in every direction.

"Hen! Mom! Mom!"

She tore through the trees, not caring which way she went. All she wanted was to get out of the woods. Her foot caught on a root, and she tumbled onto her hands and knees. She scrambled up to her feet, but the tops of the trees twirled in a rapid circle, and she fell down again. This time, the side of her head hit a rock with a sickening, dull crack. As blackness flooded over her, Izzy heard the sweet, sad music fading into the distance.

THE WITCH'S HOUSE

Izzy opened one eye and quickly shut it again. She held very still, wishing the rest of the world would do the same thing. She reached up to feel the side of her throbbing head and winced. It was painfully tender, but there wasn't any blood.

All at once, the fear came flooding back. Hen! Where was she? Izzy opened her eyes and looked around. She lay on a sofa that wasn't her own, wrapped in a checkered quilt. The room smelled like sharp cheese and freshly cut grass. She sat straight up, which instantly made her feel sick. She tried to focus on the coffee table in front of her to make the room stop spinning.

Dirty teacups, photo albums, and stacks of ancient-looking books covered the little table. The book titles were written in Latin or French or some other language Izzy didn't understand, though she could pick out a few words: *Enchantement*, *Fey*, *Magia*. Something peeking out of the pages of one of the albums caught her eye. Even though it was only the corner of a photo, she had a weird feeling she'd seen it before. She slipped the picture out of the album.

Izzy gasped. A small girl with mousy brown hair smiled back at her.

It was her own kindergarten school picture.

Her hand shaking, Izzy reached out and opened the cover of the photo album. Her school portraits covered the first page. The next sheet was dedicated to pictures of Hen. Izzy flipped the thick pages faster and faster. Ballet recitals, artwork, Christmas cards. The album was a scrapbook of her and her sister's lives. Izzy looked around the strange room. Garlands of tiny silver bells hung in the windows, just like at her grandmother's house. Where was she?

Outside, a goat bleated softly. Boots clomped over the wood floor in the next room. Izzy searched for the door. Before she could stand, Marian Malloy walked around the corner. She spotted Izzy and hurried toward the couch.

Izzy shrank away from her. "No! Stay away from me!"

The old woman stepped closer.

Izzy tried to run for the door, but the walls spun around, and she sank to the wooden floor. The next thing she knew, she lay next to the couch, covered in cold sweat, with Marian cradling her neck.

"Easy, dear, take it easy," the old woman said gruffly. "Or you'll make yourself sick all over my good rug."

She helped Izzy back to the sofa and smoothed the hair

away from her damp forehead. Izzy gave up on resisting. She felt too dizzy to move. She lay still while Marian gently took her face in her hands and turned it to the side, looking closely at her injury.

The old woman smiled, and a hundred tiny wrinkles appeared at the corners of her blue eyes. "You'll be just fine. But you'll have a devil of a headache tomorrow."

"Where's my sister?" Izzy croaked. "What did you do with her?"

"Do with her? What makes you think I did anything with her?"

Izzy pointed a trembling finger at the photo album. "You have all those pictures of us."

Marian sighed. She reached down to the album and turned it so Izzy could see the words embossed on the spine: *Jean E. Doyle*. Her grandmother's name.

"She gave it to me just before she died," said Marian.

Fighting the dizziness, Izzy sat up. "No, that's a lie. Our grandmother wouldn't have something like that. She didn't care about us. She didn't even know us."

Marian's eyes seemed to hold years of sadness. "She did care for you, child. More than you could possibly know." The old woman picked up Izzy's kindergarten photo and slid it into an empty pocket of the album. "Your grandmother told me to keep this safe. She made me promise to keep you girls safe too." She smiled again. "That'd be easier to do if you didn't go

29

around knocking your head against rocks. I found you lying in the woods, just behind my vegetable garden. Does your mother know where you are?"

Izzy felt so confused. She knew she should be afraid of Marian Malloy. The old woman was a stranger. And according to the cashier at the Jiggly Goat, she was a witch who ate children and spit out their bones. But now that Izzy sat face-to-face with her, she didn't think Marian seemed like a witch at all. At least not the child-eating kind.

Marian picked up a mug from the table and handed it to Izzy. "Drink a little. For the nausea."

Izzy took a tentative sip of the brown liquid inside. It tasted like mud with metal in it, but it instantly made her dizziness go away.

"Better?" asked Marian.

Izzy nodded and took another sip.

"That a girl. Now, let's get you back. I don't have a phone, or I'd call your mother to tell her we're on our way. Is your sister home with her?"

"No, she's lost. My sister's lost in the woods." Saying the words out loud made Izzy's throat tighten up. "We have to find her! We have to tell my mom!"

Marian squeezed her hand. "Of course we will, of course. Don't worry. She can't be far. And I could find a thimble at midnight in these woods." She helped Izzy to stand up. "I'll even bet she's already back at your house, worried about what's happened to *you*."

Izzy took a deep breath and let it out again. Maybe Hen was back at home, eating a snack at the kitchen table right now. But then Izzy remembered the music she'd heard earlier. The melody still played in her head, and it gave her a strange, uneasy feeling.

"Marian? Was that you playing the music in the woods?"

Marian's smile vanished. "*What* did you say?"

"The music. I heard music in the woods when Hen ran off."

Marian leaned down, searching Izzy's face. "Do you remember what it sounded like?"

Izzy thought for a moment. "It sounded like a flute. The music was sweet, like a happy song. But underneath the notes, I think it was actually a little sad." Izzy shut her eyes. She hummed the part of the melody that she could remember. "I think it was something like that."

When she opened her eyes again, she was shocked to see that Marian's face had turned ghostly white.

The old woman put her hands on Izzy's shoulders. Her words were slow and serious. "Did you see anyone else? A thin man with black hair?"

The thought of someone else in the woods with her sister sent a chill up Izzy's back. "No. There was no one."

"What about another child? Or an animal that seemed out of place?"

"What? No, I didn't see anything!"

Marian rubbed her chin and started pacing in front of

the door. She talked to herself, the words coming so fast Izzy could hardly catch them. "The Piper… Could it really be? But what could he be up to? He left no one in Exchange…" She stared at the photo album, cracking her knuckles over and over again. Suddenly, she jerked her head up. "September! Of course! Oh, I have to hurry!"

The old woman bolted past Izzy into the kitchen. Izzy followed after her.

Marian yanked open cabinets and started pulling everything down onto the counter. A full sack of flour tipped onto the floor, but she didn't even notice. She grabbed a canvas satchel and began stuffing jars and fistfuls of dried herbs inside.

"What else, what else…" Marian muttered. She dumped the salt out of its shaker into her palm, then let it fall to the floor. "Not enough! Shoot, there's no time to get more!"

Izzy grew increasingly anxious the more she watched the old woman. "Marian? What's going on? Is Hen all right?"

Marian snatched a jar of brown seeds off the counter and shoved it into her bag. She marched over to Izzy and patted her shoulder. She smiled, but it was a thin smile that didn't hide the worry written on her face. "I think your sister may be lost after all. But I don't want you to fret. I'm going to look for her."

"And you'll find her? Won't you?"

Marian frowned and slung the bag over her shoulder. "Come along. Let's get you home."

IN THROUGH THE
FAIRY DOOR

IZZY PANTED AS SHE followed Marian back through the woods. The old woman was right—she did know her way through the forest. It didn't take long before they stood at the edge of the Doyle property. Dublin came trotting up to them. He danced around Marian's legs a few times, then snuffled Izzy's hand happily, as if everything were perfectly normal.

Marian pointed toward Izzy's house. "You go run on now and tell your mother your sister's lost."

Izzy rubbed her temples, wishing she could think clearly. The dizziness was gone, but her brain still felt wrapped in fog. "You're not coming with me?"

Marian shook her head. "I've already lost enough time. I've got to start looking now." She squeezed Izzy's shoulder once and patted Dublin on the head. Then she turned around and strode quickly back into the woods.

"But what should I tell her?"

"Whatever you like," Marian said over her shoulder.

The words gave Izzy a sinking feeling, like it didn't matter what she said. She watched until Marian disappeared back into the trees, then turned to head to her own house. When Izzy rounded the boulder pile, she saw Hen's sparkly back-pack at the base of the rocks. The zipper gaped open. As Izzy reached down to pick it up, she saw two packages of cheese crackers and two sandwich bags poking out of the jumble of plastic toys. She pulled out the sandwiches. Hen had made one of them with honey, not jelly. Just the way Izzy liked it.

She zipped the sandwiches back up and slung the back-pack over her shoulder. But instead of walking back home, she stood there with her forehead leaning against the cool sand-stone boulders. Dublin worked his wet nose into her hand.

"Why are you in such a good mood?" she whispered, let-ting him lick her fingers.

Izzy felt sick all over again, but not from the bruise on her head. She knew she should be running for home, screaming for her mom to call the police. But something deep in the center of her chest told her that no police search would ever find Hen. She looked over her shoulder at the trees behind her. Marian said she needed to start looking right away. But how could the old woman search the entire woods all by her-self? Izzy shut her eyes and let the melody of that strange, sad music come back to her.

The music had meant something to Marian. She didn't

seem worried about Hen at all until Izzy hummed the song for her. What was the name she used? *The Piper.*

Clarity suddenly snapped through the fog wrapped around Izzy's brain.

Hen wasn't lost. She had been kidnapped.

And Marian knew exactly who did it.

Izzy turned around. A shiver of fear raced up her arms as she started retracing her steps back into the woods. She had never been in a forest by herself until today. In fact, she'd never been in a forest at all, unless you counted strolling along the paved trails of a nature preserve. But this time, Dublin stayed by her side, and there was no strange music, only the light ruffling of wind through the leaves.

Izzy moved carefully through the brambly undergrowth. She didn't want to trip and fall again. She also didn't want Marian to know she was following her. The old woman would tell Izzy to get on back home, and then she'd never figure out what was really going on.

Deeper into the woods, Izzy spotted the old woman on the other side of a leaf-covered gully. She stopped and pressed Dublin's rump onto the ground.

"You sit here, and don't move a muscle," she whispered to him. She crouched down and summoned up her special trick.

It was a talent she'd discovered during hide-and-seek games with Hen. She would imagine she was a fox, stalking an unsuspecting bird. She placed each foot on the ground with silent precision, quiet as a padded paw. She looked back at Dublin, expecting him to follow her or start whining. But he sat as still as a stone, as if she had given him orders in his own language.

Marian walked slowly, her eyes trained on the ground. She stopped once, scratching her head and muttering to herself. She bent to the ground and brushed aside the leaves. The old woman dug her finger into the soil and put it to her lips, like someone tasting the icing on a cake. She stood up, changed her direction a little, and kept walking.

Izzy crept closer, as foxlike and silent as she could manage, until Marian came to a stop in front of a boulder beside a bent oak tree. Marian paused and looked over her shoulder. Izzy ducked down behind a bush and held absolutely still, peeking over the top.

The old woman tasted the ground once more and then began to pace slowly around the stone and the tree. She circled them twice and walked behind them again. This time, she didn't emerge on the other side.

Izzy stayed crouched for what seemed like an eternity, waiting for Marian to reappear. But she never did. Izzy stood up and walked to the other side of the boulder. Nothing. She walked around the stone and the tree three times, just as Marian had. Still nothing.

Izzy clucked her tongue to call Dublin over. She stood with her hands on her hips, while he sniffed the ground at her feet. Had the old woman somehow slipped away without her seeing? She was about to give up and go searching in another direction, when Dublin started whining at something on the ground.

"Hush, boy!"

Izzy knelt beside him and put her arm around his neck to settle him down. He sniffed at a round pad of moss the size of a dinner plate. Though the rest of the ground was dry, tiny droplets of water trembled on the feathery leaves. Izzy pressed one finger into the spongy pad. She pulled her hand back as a thick chunk of moss fell away, revealing a dark, gaping hole in the ground. Using both hands, she peeled away the rest of the moss and leaned over the hole.

Izzy picked up a pebble and dropped it down the hole. She heard a soft thud, followed by another much farther down. As she lowered her face over the darkness, the sound of her own breath echoed back at her. A draft of cool air flowed onto her face. It smelled fresh and a little sweet, like honeysuckles. Her pupils dilated, and she could see a very faint green light at the bottom.

This wasn't a hole in the ground. It was a passage.

Sweat beaded up on Izzy's forehead. This was insane. Was she really about to follow a complete stranger down a dark tunnel in the ground? She should go home, get her mom, call the police. But Izzy knew if she left, she'd never be able to find this spot in the woods again. Then what would happen to Hen?

Izzy bit down on her cheek until it hurt. This whole thing was her fault. If only she'd gotten out of bed earlier or not finished that stupid crossword puzzle, Hen might be at home right now, twirling around the living room. Izzy felt a whisper-thin thread still connected her to her sister, and it ran right down into that dark tunnel. She felt sure that if she walked away, the thread might snap forever, and she'd never see Hen again.

Dublin whimpered beside her.

"Don't worry, Dub. I'll be right back, OK?"

She sat down and let her feet slide over the edge of the hole. The damp earth scraped against her legs as she lowered herself down. To her surprise, the hole wasn't nearly as small as it looked. She had to shrug off Hen's backpack and let it slide down behind her, but otherwise, she slipped inside easily.

The tunnel sloped steeply toward the green light at the other end. Damp soil caked up under her palms and elbows as she slid down, a few inches at a time. Halfway down, she stopped and looked up at the way she came. The silhouette of Dublin's blocky head loomed above the opening of the passage. She continued, while the light grew brighter with every inch. Another draft of the cool, fragrant air fluttered upward, ruffling the hair at her temples.

When she reached the bottom of the tunnel, she huddled there like a fox in its den, waiting to feel the courage to make her go forward. Instead, she had an overwhelming desire to run back home. *You can't stop now. You've come this far*, she told herself.

With a deep breath, she moved forward into the blinding green light.

NETHERBEE HALL

IZZY SET HER FEET down and stood up. She looked around, confused. She was still in the woods. Directly behind her stood an enormous tree whose branches twisted overhead, out of sight. Its trunk was as big around as her family's dining room table. A large hole gaped open in its center.

Izzy braced her hands against the tree and leaned into the hole. It was pitch-black inside the trunk and smelled of wet earth and mushrooms. She could hear Dublin's whimper echoing from somewhere in the darkness. Her stomach fluttered anxiously as she looked around again.

At first, she'd thought she had stumbled into a different patch of the same woods. But now, she realized the trees were different. They looked like the same ones growing near her house, but they were all double the size. Sunlight filtered down through their leaves, casting everything in a green-tinted shade.

Izzy waited for the goose bumps to stop running up the backs of her arms. She stood on a narrow dirt path. There was no sign of Marian. To the right, the path wound through the woods and out of sight. To the left, it curled around a magnolia tree with white blossoms the size of soup bowls. Izzy walked until she could see around the magnolia's trunk. The path ran straight toward a pair of wooden doors set in a high stone wall. One of the doors stood slightly ajar.

Izzy approached the wall slowly. This had to be a dream. Maybe she had fallen and hit her head again. She tapped her fingers against her cheeks to see if that would wake her up. Nothing happened, and now she stood just inches from the great wooden doors. Rough-cut carvings danced across the shiny wood. Izzy traced a finger over the image of a farmer and a king, their hands clasped in greeting. A border of strange animals framed the two figures. Some of the animals had children's faces. They grinned at Izzy impishly, like they might nibble her fingers. She pushed on one of the doors, and it groaned open to reveal an overgrown courtyard, and beyond that, a large, gray house.

"Marian?" Izzy whispered. She stepped through the doorway into the courtyard. "Hello?"

The entire place was silent. Izzy stepped over the weeds poking through the pavers. Her eyes traveled up to the house. Splotches of moss and lichen covered the walls. It looked like no one had lived there in a very long time. Izzy walked up the steps to the front door. It stood open just an inch. She reached out to pull the handle. A hand shot out through the open crack, grabbed her arm, and wrenched her inside.

Izzy's scream rang off the walls of a dark room. She felt callused fingers clamp down over her mouth.

"Hush, child! Stop that wailing, or I'll stuff a kerchief in your mouth!"

Izzy's eyes adjusted to the darkness, and she saw Marian's wrinkled face glowering down at her.

"What on earth are you doing here?" Marian whispered. She released her grip on Izzy. "How'd you find this place? I was very careful the whole way here!"

"I—I followed you through the woods," said Izzy.

Marian raised her eyebrows. "Humph, you'd have to be quieter than a mouse to follow me."

Izzy swung her gaze from the old woman to the rest of the house. They stood in a large entry hall in front of a long staircase. The stair railing lay broken on the steps. Dried leaves covered the dusty floor, and gauzy, white cobwebs settled into every corner.

Marian grabbed Izzy by the elbow and started to pull her back toward the front door. "If you came down that passage, then you can go right back up it. You're going straight home, you hear?"

Izzy yanked her arm away. "No, I'm not going back until you tell me what's going on! Where's Hen? What is this place?"

"This is Netherbee Hall," said Marian. "Or it was anyway."

"And Hen is here?"

"Does it look like anyone's here to you?"

"Well, where is she then? You said you were going to find her."

"He must have taken her straight to the city," said Marian, more to herself than to Izzy. "It'll take him two days to get there. I wonder if he still rides that horse of his…"

Izzy was tired of Marian's secrets. "You know something you're not telling me! How do I know *you* didn't kidnap Hen in the first place?"

"Child, you know as well as me that I didn't take your sister," the old woman snapped. "I came into Faerie to find her."

"Faerie?" asked Izzy. "You mean *Faerie*? Like in the books?"

"Yes. And no, not like in the books. Not your books, at any rate."

"No… That's not possible…"

Izzy cast her eyes around the room, looking for something to prove to her she wasn't standing in a magical world.

Marian stared down at the floor, cracking her knuckles. Slowly, she raised her eyes to meet Izzy's. "What did the folks back in Everton tell you about me?"

"The cashier at the grocery store said you were a witch."

"Pah, don't I wish. Only humans are witches."

Izzy gulped and took a step back. "Wait—what do you mean?"

Marian took off her hat and brushed her hair behind her ears. Izzy gasped. They were pointed.

A CHILD FOR A
CHANGELING

Izzy stared at Marian. The old woman's ears weren't just a little pointy. The tops swept up into tall peaks that nearly extended past her head.

"What *are* you?"

Marian held her gaze. "Your grandmother once told me you liked to read fairy tales. Then you must know that when the fairies take a human child, they always leave someone in its place."

Izzy knew exactly what Marian was talking about. One of her favorite stories from *Faerie and Folktales of Yesteryear* was an Irish tale. In it, the parents looked into their baby's crib only to find it wasn't their baby at all but a shape-shifter that had taken its place.

"A Changeling," Izzy whispered.

She watched in amazement as the old woman's ears shrank smaller and smaller. The long, pointed tips softened and rounded until they looked just like a pair of normal, human ears.

"Just about the only part of me that'll still Change," said Marian, plopping the hat back on her head. "Been stuck in this form too long."

Izzy tapped her cheeks again, harder this time. She'd given up thinking she was dreaming, but she couldn't quite make herself believe this was all real either. A breeze fluttered in through one of the broken windows. Izzy glanced at the trees outside.

Trees at the bottom of a hole in the ground.

Izzy gulped. "Marian, what is going on? And what does any of this have to do with my sister?"

The old woman turned around and walked to the far end of the entry hall. She stopped at the foot of a dark painting on the wall. The colors had begun to turn black, but Izzy could still make out the figures. It was the same farmer and king she had seen carved into the wooden doors outside. The round-eared farmer held a scythe in one hand. The king's crown rested on his long, pointed ears. A dozen animals with children's faces danced in a circle around their feet.

Marian gazed up at the portrait with her fingers clasped behind her back. "The last time I was here was sixty years ago. I hardly recognize this place; it was so different then. Full of fairies coming and going between your world and ours. A few humans too, though trade was already starting to slow down in my time. Now, it looks like it's dried up altogether."

The old woman turned around and smiled like she was lost in a daydream. "I stood in this very spot, waiting for the Piper to take me up to Earth. I was so nervous! Scared to death I wouldn't be able to hold my form or that I wouldn't do a good job of fitting in." Marian laughed, and then her smile faded. "Guess I had a reason to be nervous. I never did fit in.

"I wouldn't have lasted if it hadn't been for your grandmother," she continued. "Jean and I grew up together. She was my only friend. Even when I told her I was a fairy, she didn't care one bit." Marian sighed sadly. "So now you understand why I knew about the music you heard in the woods. It's the same song the Piper played all those years ago when he took me to Earth for the Exchange."

"Exchange? You mean the Piper steals people's children without them knowing," said Izzy. "That's horrible."

The old woman exhaled out the side of her mouth. "It's complicated. You're a human. You wouldn't understand."

"So you switched places with the real Marian Malloy?" asked Izzy. "What happened to her?"

"Human children are adopted by fairy families. She's probably living her life somewhere out there, with a whole mess of part-fairy grandchildren hanging around her skirts."

The full weight of what Marian was saying finally hit Izzy. Her throat clenched tighter. "But if the Piper took my sister, that means some fairy family is going to adopt her too. But she already has a family. She has us!"

Marian took Izzy's hands in hers. "I tried so hard to prevent this. Everton's a border town between our worlds. Even now, lots of fairy roads still run through it. That makes it an easy target for the Exchange. I taught Jean every precaution to keep her children from being taken. The bells, the stone towers—they're all signals to the Piper, to keep him away. It worked for your father, but when you were born, I told Jean never to let you come back to her house. You were so little, and there was something different about you. The Piper looks for the different ones. You see, your grandmother didn't push you away because she didn't love you. She wanted to keep you safe."

"And what about Hen?" asked Izzy, her voice trembling. "Is she safe? When the Piper takes a child, does he ever let them go?"

Marian frowned. "I don't know. But I'm going to do all I can to make him." A spark of hope glinted in her eye. "He didn't leave your family with anyone in Exchange, and that's against the rules. *A Child for a Changeling*, that's the old promise. If I can catch up to him, I think I can argue a good case for returning her."

"Where do you think he took her?"

"If she's not here, there's only one other place she can be." Marian pointed toward the front door. "That path out there leads straight through the Edgewood, to Avhalon—"

"Avalon! Like the island from the story of King Arthur?"

"Yes and no. King Arthur was just a made-up character, but *Avhalon* is real. And it isn't an island. It's a city. The Piper took your sister there. I'm sure of it." Marian cupped Izzy's chin in her rough hand. "You must trust me, child. I won't rest till she's back safe."

Izzy bit back her tears. The day had turned from reality to dream to nightmare almost too fast for her to bear. But Marian's steely determination gave her hope. Izzy squeezed her hand. "I trust you."

Another breeze blew in through the windows, sweeping the brittle leaves across the floor.

"Come on," said Marian. She put her hand on Izzy's back and directed her to the front doors. "We need to get you home, and I need to be on my way—"

They stopped and stared at the wooden doors. Both were covered in a thick, white mat of cobwebs.

"They weren't like that before, were they?" asked Izzy, taking a step back.

She looked down at her feet. Though she couldn't see any spiders, the webs spread steadily across the floor toward them, reaching out wispy tentacles.

Izzy kicked at the cobwebs. Several tendrils whipped around her ankle and pulled it forward, knocking her off balance. The old woman caught her arm. She drew a dirty knife from its case on her belt and sliced through the webs. They dissolved like smoke, only to be replaced by a dozen more that lurched hungrily for Izzy's legs. She jerked her foot away from them and staggered back.

Marian pulled her away from the doors. "Not this way! We'll find another way out!"

They turned to head down the hall but stopped again. The

cobwebs had already crawled up the walls and knitted themselves into a pulsating curtain of lace that completely blocked the hallway.

"Up the stairs!" cried Marian, dragging Izzy by the arm.

They bolted up the crumbling steps, tripping over broken pieces of stone. Izzy looked over her shoulder. The entire floor where they had stood was now a solid sheet of white. The cobwebs writhed up the walls toward them. The portrait of the farmer and king disappeared under a thick film of gauze. At the top of the stairs, they turned to the left and ran down another long hall. They ducked into a large room to their right. Marian leaned against the heavy door, slamming it shut.

Izzy looked around the empty room. How long would the door hold back the cobwebs? There was no other way out that she could see.

Marian knelt down and opened her satchel. "I must have brought something that can ward them off!" She started pulling out glass jars and bottles and hurriedly read the labels. "*Thistle Thwart*, no… *Prune Prepare*…no, that won't work either!"

Izzy bent down and picked through the jars, but she didn't know what Marian was looking for. From the labels, they all seemed to be meant for the garden.

"What about this?" she asked, holding up a small, cloudy blue bottle. "It says *Root Revive*."

"No, no!" said Marian. "That's just for dead trees."

"Marian!" Izzy jumped up and backed away from the door. "Get up! Look!"

Cobwebs probed through the crack. Izzy shoved the bottle into her pocket. She took off the backpack and whacked at them until they retreated. She stood staring at the door, her chest heaving. A single web licked at the crack. In an instant, a hundred others joined it.

"To the window!" ordered Marian, abandoning her satchel.

They fled across the stone floor to the far side of the room. The center windowpane had been smashed long ago, and Marian kicked at the broken glass until she cleared it away from the windowsill.

"Give me your hands," she told Izzy. "I'll lower you down, and you wait for me at the bottom."

Izzy hung her legs over the window ledge. Behind Marian, the cobwebs completely covered the door and one of the walls. They spilled toward them across the floor.

"Go on. I'll jump down after you." Marian took both of Izzy's hands and lowered her down, leaning far over the edge of the windowsill.

Izzy placed her feet on the wall of the building to steady herself. At the count of three, Marian let go of her hands, and she fell hard onto the ground. She leapt up to her feet and waited for Marian to climb out after her.

"Oh, please hurry!" Izzy shouted.

Marian shook her head. "It's too far for me to jump."

"What? No! I can't go without you!"

"Don't worry about me," Marian shouted. "Just go on!"

The window to the right of Marian filmed over with cob-webs as if it were frosted with snow. The old woman looked over her shoulder and then ran to another window at her left.

"Get out of here, child!" she shouted, her voice muffled by the glass. "Go on!"

With a crack, the front doors of the house burst open, and an enormous mass of cobwebs cascaded out onto the court-yard. Izzy bolted across the pavers to the doors in the wall and pushed them open.

Marian beat at the window until she knocked a hole in the brittle glass. "The path!" she called through the broken pane. "Don't leave that path, whatever you do!"

Marian turned her back to the window and slid down out of Izzy's sight. The window clouded over with white. She was gone.

Thick waves of cobwebs rolled out over the courtyard toward Izzy. Within seconds, she would be submerged beneath them. She ran through the doors, the white strands licking at her heels. Her foot caught the doorframe, sending her flying onto her stomach. She rolled over to see the mass of cobwebs undulating toward her. Izzy scrambled to her feet and tore off running down the path, not daring to look back.

THE ROCK THAT WASN'T

IZZY KEPT RUNNING EVEN though her lungs begged her to slow down. The backpack bounced against her spine, jangling the plastic toys inside. The icy touch of the cobwebs still lingered on her skin. She felt sure that, at any moment, a white tidal wave would come crashing down the path behind her and swallow her up.

Izzy didn't slow down until she came to a dead tree that had fallen across a bend in the path. She stood beside the log, hands on her knees, wheezing for air. She looked back at the way she just came. No cobwebs. The forest was still except for the light rustle of leaves overhead. She took a deep breath and let it out slowly, trying to decide what to do.

The hole in the tree trunk that led back to her home—back to her *world*—was long gone. She'd sprinted past it during her escape. Finding it again meant going back to Netherbee Hall, back to the cobwebs. Even if she could make it, what would she do when she got back home? What would she tell her parents? That their youngest daughter was kidnapped by a fairy? That her rescuer now lay cocooned in a shroud of cobwebs? They'd never believe it. Izzy could hardly believe it herself.

She shuddered and closed her eyes. How could this be happening? Faerie was real. Changelings were real. The stories she'd read and loved were true. Things should have been wonderful. Instead, this was the worst thing that had ever happened.

Izzy looked up into the forest canopy. She couldn't tell the sun's position, but she guessed it must be late afternoon. She definitely did not want to spend the night in these woods. She placed her hands on the fallen tree and looked down the path snaking ahead of her. Marian said it led straight to Avhalon, where the Piper would take Hen to be adopted. Izzy tugged down on the backpack straps. She had to find the Piper and tell him this was all a huge mistake. Hen already had a family. Surely, he would understand and let her go.

Izzy planted a foot on top of the log. She was just about to climb over it when she heard a noise. It sounded like someone crying.

Izzy scanned the trees, listening. She heard it again—a low whimper. Fifty feet ahead of her, a large, mossy boulder sat in the center of the path. The crying seemed to be coming from that direction. She stared at the boulder, ready to run if she had to.

The rock moved.

Izzy ducked to the ground, her heart racing. Slowly, she rose up on her knees until she could just see over the top of the log. The boulder sighed. It began to heave up and down, making pitiful sobbing sounds.

Izzy blinked her eyes over and over. The boulder wasn't a boulder at all but some sort of creature who sat hunched over on the path with its back to her. Its shabby tunic and trousers were so pilled and nubby that she'd mistaken them for moss. The creature reached up its large hands to its face as if it were wiping away tears, revealing arms covered in dark-brown hair.

"Oh dear, oh dear." The creature's low voice cracked as he sniffled. "I'm in for it now."

In a burst of energy, he stood up. He strained with all his might, pulling on his hairy leg with both hands. As he struggled, Izzy saw a thin silver chain wound around his ankle, secured at the other end to a stake in the ground. Despite his great size, he couldn't free his leg from the delicate chain. He collapsed on the path again, breathing hard. Then he pushed himself up onto his hands and feet and did something that made Izzy's mouth drop wide open.

It started with a shiver of his shoulder muscles. His back billowed up and became covered with thick fur. He arched his back, tilting his face to the sky. His flat nose stretched into a thick snout. His pointed ears rounded and shifted to the top of his head. It was like he had melted from one creature into something completely different. Now, he was a scraggly, brown bear. His tattered clothes were gone, but the silver chain remained. He gnawed at it with his jaws, but it was no use.

The bear changed again, this time into a shaggy sort of ram that stamped its hooves and jerked at the chain. The ram then became an ox, and next an overgrown badger. Izzy forgot to breathe as she watched him transform from one animal to the next with ease. But no matter what he did, the chain held tight. Finally, looking very exhausted, he changed back into his first form and resumed his whimpering, his head in his hands.

Izzy made a conscious effort to close her mouth. If she hadn't already seen a hundred other unbelievable things that day, she'd tell herself she was hallucinating. The creature must be a Changeling, just like Marian. So did that mean he would be friendly? Or did it mean he was somehow connected to the Piper? Izzy still didn't understand if the Piper was good or not. She wished more than anything that Marian was still with her.

The creature sighed mournfully. It reminded Izzy of Dublin whimpering when they left him home alone. Whatever he was, she couldn't just leave him there to suffer.

She stood up and climbed over the log. As she approached the creature, she smoothed her hair forward to cover up her ears. Until she knew more about him, she wanted to keep her humanness a secret.

Izzy tiptoed forward until she was just a few yards away. "Excuse me, um, sir?"

The creature sat up and turned his head back and forth. "Who's—who's there?" he called.

"Ahem. Excuse me, but—"

He turned and locked eyes with Izzy. "Aaah! Oh dear, oh dear! This is the end! How did it all come to this? Make it quick then, and just slice my throat!" He flopped down onto his back, and his round belly shook with sobs.

"Slice your throat? No, no, I'm not going to do anything like that! I was going to ask if you wanted me to try and help you. That's all."

"Then this isn't your trap? You're not working for the Unglers?"

"The who?" asked Izzy, walking forward. "I don't know what you're talking about. But if you hold still, I could try to look at that chain."

"It's useless," he said as he snuffled, swinging his leg out so she could see. "The snare's absolutely unbreakable. You'll have to leave me here, unless you want to be caught yourself."

Izzy glanced out into the forest. It was so peaceful at the moment. Surely, there was time to set him free. "Let's see what I can do."

She bent closer to his ankle. Blood soaked the creature's thick hair where the snare cut into his skin. It was knotted in a noose that got tighter the more one struggled, perfect for catching something large and clumsy. Izzy worked on the knot very patiently, testing it first one way and then another. It reminded her of untangling her necklaces after Hen made a mess of them.

As she worked, she stole a glance up at the creature. He

wasn't an animal, but he wasn't quite a person either. Fine, downy fur covered his flat face, which was dark brown as garden soil except for a black stripe that ran across his eyes like a burglar's mask. He had a velvety nose, just like Dublin's, and a thin-lipped mouth. His large eyes held a childlike sweetness, but he was too big to be called a boy. He looked like he'd be at least as tall as Izzy's dad.

"I should never have come to Hollowdell," he said with a sniffle. "It's too near the Road. But it's gumroot season, and this is the best place to find them." He nodded toward a basket lying just to the side of the path full of plump, dark-purple tubers with leafy green tops. "I was just about to be off for home when I see the biggest, fattest gumroot. I go to pick it up, and *snap!* I'm caught. I should've known there'd be snares here—Selden even warned me of it—but did I listen? Learned my lesson now though, I can tell you that. Well, say…look there!"

The loops of chain now hung looser around his ankle. Izzy was only a few more maneuvers away from releasing his foot when she heard a piercing shriek echo through the woods.

"It's the Unglers!" whispered the creature, wringing his hands. "And me without my Stairstep! Oh, if they smell me, I'm done for!"

Izzy worked her fingers faster. "Almost got it…"

The shrieks grew louder and were joined by others. They sounded like pigs squealing, but from the terrified look on the creature's face, Izzy knew they must be something much worse.

"Oh, please hurry—they're getting closer!" he cried.

"Almost. One more second. There!"

The creature stood up and flexed his foot. "A thousand, thousand thanks, friend!" He grabbed her hand and shook it up and down vigorously. "But let's be out of here, quick!" He fetched his basket and started bounding into the woods. "Come on!" he called over his shoulder.

Izzy stood frozen to the spot. "But—the path! I'm not supposed to leave it!" she shouted after him.

"Don't be foolish!" he said, turning and coming back to her. "Don't you hear them?"

The screeching sounded closer every second. Izzy wasn't sure what was louder—the shrieks or Marian's voice ringing in her ears, warning her to stay on the path no matter what.

"The Unglers can pluck the flesh right off your bones!" said the creature, his dark eyes growing even wider. "They'll start with your kneecaps!"

That settled it. She wasn't going to stand around waiting for something to eat her knees. With a running leap, she left the path and landed in the thick moss at the creature's feet.

"Finally! Thought you'd never come to your senses," he said. "Let's get moving. Up you go!"

He bent down and picked her up under the arms, hoisting her onto his shoulders. Before she could say anything else, he took off crashing through the brushy understory.

Behind them, the path receded from view and disappeared.

10

THROUGH THE EDGEWOOD

THE CREATURE DIDN'T STOP until they reached the edge of a stony creek. "Here we are, and down you go." He lifted Izzy off his shoulders and set her gently on the ground. He waded into the water, wriggling his leathery toes. "Ah... Nothing like a cold soak after a long hike, I always say. Go on, have a dip if you like. My name's Lug. What's yours?"

"Um, Isabella," said Izzy, looking around nervously. "What if the Unglers saw us come this way?"

"They can't see," said Lug. "Haven't got any eyes. Besides, this is miles from the Road, and they never stray far from it."

"Wait. Do you mean we're miles from the path?"

Lug sat down on the stream bank and carefully inspected the gumroots in his basket. "Hmm? Oh yes, far, far away from it, thank goodness."

Tears welled up in Izzy's eyes. Not even one hour in Faerie and she had already gone against Marian's advice. She was more lost than she could possibly be, and not a single soul knew where she was or how to find her. She would never, ever find Hen now.

Lug hurried to her and wrapped her in his long arms. It stopped her from crying—mostly because he was pressing her so tightly into his warm belly that she could hardly breathe.

"There, there, my girl. I know that was all a bit frightening, but we're safe now. Here, have a gumroot. They're better roasted, but they're not too bad raw either. That's a girl... Er, what did you say your name was again?"

"Call me Izzy," she answered, taking one of the purple roots from Lug. Her first thought was to refuse it—what if it made her turn into a toad or something horrible like that? But Lug looked at her so expectantly. She nibbled the crunchy root. It tasted like beets mixed with licorice.

Lug's smile spread the length of his wide face. "There you go, Izzy! You'll feel better as soon as you get some gumroot in your belly. Being hungry is enough to make anyone upset. Go have a seat, and I'll look around for some tipplewort. The two go together perfectly."

Izzy sat on a flat rock near the edge of the stream while Lug waded to the other side, searching the banks. He soon came back with his hands full of bundles of tender green shoots. They sat side by side, taking alternating bites of the gumroot and the juicy tipplewort, which fizzed in Izzy's mouth like ginger ale.

"Go easy on that stuff, now," said Lug. "It can make you a little loopy if you eat too much of it at once."

Without the empty feeling in her stomach, Izzy did start to feel better. She looked up at her strange new companion. Her mind burned with a thousand questions for him. Where were they? How far was Avhalon? Did he know anything that could help her find Hen? But she worried those questions would make him ask questions of his own, and she wasn't sure how to answer them. Her gut told her that she could trust Lug. After all, he'd helped her get away from the Unglers, who didn't sound like anyone she'd want to meet.

"Lug, how do the Unglers set their traps if they can't see?" she asked.

Lug waggled his fingers over her face. "They've got horrid, clever hands. Almost like they have eyes on each fingertip. And when they've caught something"—he tapped his nose—"they can smell it a mile away."

Izzy shuddered at the description. "Have you ever been caught by them before?"

"Goodness, no! If I had, I'd be—" Lug caught himself and turned to look at her. "Say, you must not be from the Edgewood if you don't know about the Unglers." His eyes scanned her clothes and backpack. "You some sort of vagabond peddler?"

Izzy patted her hair to make sure her ears were still concealed. "I'm just…you know…traveling through."

"Where to?"

"To…the city." Izzy held her breath, hoping she sounded believable.

"Oh, to Avhalon? Splendid!"

She exhaled with relief. "Have you been there?"

"Used to live there," he said proudly. "Best days of my life were spent in Avhalon. Would love to be journeying there myself." He looked up wistfully at the trees. "You must be going to the Apple Festival."

Izzy tried to remember what Marian had said about Avhalon. She couldn't recall anything about a festival, but it sounded like a good enough reason to be on her way to a fairy city. "I'm going to…to meet my sister there."

"What lucky girls! This is the first festival they've had in years. But you shouldn't be on the City Road, you know. It's full of dangers. Not just the Unglers—bandits, bogies, all sorts of nasty things."

Izzy frowned. Faerie must have changed since Marian left, or she would have warned her about those things. "But someone once told me never to leave the path—I mean, the Road. She acted like if I didn't stay on it, I'd never find my way out of the woods."

"Oh yes, that's true as well. Really the best thing is not to go into the Edgewood at all if you can help it."

"But don't you live here?"

"Sure." He pointed upstream. "Just up there a ways."

"Well, how do *you* keep from getting lost?"

"Oh, that took ages. Still do get lost every now and then,

especially in the winter when everything looks the same. But for now, it's much easier getting around. See this gumroot? It only grows in certain areas of the forest. There's lots of other plants like that—they only like to grow in certain places. So if I'm ever lost, I just look down, dig around a little, take a nibble of a root here or there, and I can usually figure it out."

Izzy's hopes lifted. "Do you think you could tell me how to get to Avhalon?"

"Sure I could. You know what yellow mallow looks like? In a couple days, the yellow mallow will be in bloom, and you can follow it west till you get to a cluster of old trundle oaks…"

"Maybe it would be better if you *showed* me the way," Izzy interrupted.

Lug shook his head and muttered, "Oh no, couldn't do that, I'm afraid. Couldn't do that at all." He stuffed his mouth full of tipplewort and two huge gumroots.

Izzy wondered what she'd said to make him go quiet. She sighed and looked down at the gumroot in her hand. Learning all the species of plants in the forest would take her years. If she was going to find Hen, she'd have to be more direct.

"Lug, can I ask you about something? Back there when you were still caught in the trap, I saw you transform into some different animals."

He stopped chewing and gave her a sidelong glance. "Saw that, did you?"

"Yes, I did."

"Listen, I'd appreciate it if we could keep that our little secret," he said, lowering his voice. "It's just that I'm not supposed to let anyone see me do that—"

"See you do *what*?"

They spun around to see a girl standing in the reeds behind them with her hands on her hips and a very disapproving look on her face. Lug didn't seem surprised to see her at all. He stood up quickly and brushed the tipplewort off his chin.

"Oh hello, Dree! I was just—um—talking to my friend here…"

"Your *friend*?" she asked skeptically, walking toward them.

The girl looked a couple years older than Izzy. She wore a thin dress that might have been white once upon a time but was now a smudgy gray with tattered sleeves, one of which kept slipping down off her bony shoulder. As she came closer, Izzy wondered if the tipplewort really was going to her head. No, she knew what she saw. The girl was *translucent*. Izzy could look straight through her body—clothes and all—and see the forest behind her.

The ghost-girl shot her a harsh look. "What are *you* staring at?" Without waiting for an answer, she turned to Lug again. "Have you been doing something you shouldn't?"

"No…not exactly…"

"Be honest! *Have you?*"

The girl's piercing stare was all it took to make Lug spill the entire story of their meeting. Though Izzy noticed he left off the part about hearing the Unglers' shrieks in the distance.

At the end of his tale, he said, "So you see, Dree, it really wasn't my fault! And Izzy here is a very kind girl and wouldn't dare tell anyone what she saw, I'm sure. Would you, Izzy?"

"No, I won't tell anyone. I promise," said Izzy.

Dree let out an exasperated sigh and brushed a lanky strand of dark hair out of her face. "Lug, do you realize what you've done? What if she's a *spy*?" She nodded toward Izzy without looking at her.

"Me? I'm not a spy," said Izzy.

"See?" said Lug.

"You can't expect her to admit she's a spy, can you?"

"Now why would a spy put her own life at risk to save me?" asked Lug.

"Spies will do anything to make you think they're not spies," said Dree, rolling her eyes.

"I'm *not* a spy!"

"She's going to the festival in Avhalon," explained Lug. "And I really don't think she's a spy. Look at her—she's such a little thing. We can just let her go on her way, and there's no need to tell—"

"We'll have to tell Selden, of course," said Dree, crossing her arms.

Lug clapped his hands together in front of him. "Please, oh please, Dree! Let's not tell Selden—he'll be so upset with me!"

"*I'm* upset! You know better than to go to Hollowdell on your own!"

Lug dropped his chin to his chest.

Dree let out a deep breath. She reached for one of his hands, clasping it as solidly as a normal person. "I'm sorry, but I just don't want anything bad to happen to you. You know we have to tell Selden. If he found out that someone had seen you doing *you know what*, then we let her go… Well, imagine how disappointed he'd be."

"Oh, all right," said Lug. "Let's just get it over with then."

While Dree chewed at a fingernail, Lug bent down and gathered up his basket, which was much emptier than it had been before.

"Am I going with you?" Izzy asked him in a whisper.

"Looks like it. Really sorry about all this. You know *I* don't think you're a spy."

"But where are we going?"

"Back home—our home, that is. It's not too far. Just up the stream a few miles or so."

"She'll have to be blindfolded," said Dree, taking her fingernail out of her mouth and crossing her arms again.

Izzy spun around. "Blindfolded! You really think that's necessary?"

Dree finally met her eyes. "We've got to keep our location a secret."

"And how do I know you won't throw me off a cliff once the blindfold's on?"

"Ha! There are no cliffs around here, silly!" said Lug with

a low, booming laugh. "Besides, you can ride on my shoulders again, so you know nothing bad will happen to you. The blindfold is just a formality."

"You don't need to be so paranoid," said Izzy. "I couldn't find my way around this forest if my life depended on it—which it probably does."

Neither of them had a blindfold, so she searched through Hen's backpack and found a navy silk scarf. Dree doubled up the scarf several times and tied it around Izzy's eyes. Then she helped her up onto Lug's shoulders.

Izzy swayed from side to side as Lug lumbered along. She could still hear the stream burbling to her right. She soon gave up trying to keep track of their direction. The two fairies were carrying her deeper into the forest and farther from the path, and there was nothing she could do about it.

She leaned over and spoke into Lug's ear. "Who is Selden?"

"One of my dearest friends. Don't worry. He's very nice."

"Not *all* your friends are nice," grumbled Izzy.

Lug lowered his voice. "Dree's really not so bad, you know. She's just a little stern about rules, that's all."

"I can hear you," called Dree from up ahead.

Lug dropped into a whisper. "Just like a thistle—wants to act thorny, but on the inside, soft as a feather."

"I can *still* hear you."

"And excellent ears too!"

11

YAWNING TOP

"AH, HOME AT LAST," said Lug. "Welcome to Yawning Top."

Izzy still held tight to the top of his head. She smelled a faint whiff of something rancid and wondered where in the world they'd brought her. She reached one hand up and pulled the blindfold down to her chin. They stood in front of the most enormous tree she'd ever seen. She didn't think twenty people holding hands could get their arms around it. The deeply furrowed trunk looked like ten trees fused together, stretching up toward branches that soared above the canopy, out of sight. Thousands of bright-red mushrooms covered the bark, sticking straight out like little shelves.

The creek they'd been following curled around the base of the tree trunk. Izzy heard a rustle in the reeds at the water's edge. A sleek, black stoat parted the grass, two speckled birds clamped in its teeth. When it saw them, it dropped the birds and looked up at Lug.

"Either you've grown a girl-shaped tumor," said the stoat, nodding up at Izzy, "or you've brought someone home with you. I really hope it's the first one."

Lug wrung his hands guiltily. "Selden, I can explain…"

"You know her blindfold's off, right?"

A flash of white zipped in front of Izzy's face, and a butterfly landed on the ground at Lug's feet. The butterfly grew larger as it beat its wings once, twice, and then the wings became not wings at all but the arms of a skinny girl.

"Drat!" said Dree, stamping her bare foot. "I knew I should have cinched that thing down tighter."

Lug reached up and took hold of Izzy under her arms. He set her gently on the ground beside him, while Dree glared hatefully at her.

The stoat stood up on his hind legs. "Whoa, whoa, whoa. You're Changing in front of a stranger? Will someone tell me what's going on?"

"She's already seen it," said Dree, rolling her eyes. "She saw Lug Change back in Hollowdell."

The stoat narrowed his eyes and pointed one finger at Lug. "*Hollowdell?* How many times have I said—"

"Yes, and I'm very sorry. But look—" Lug bent down and picked up his basket. "Look at this load of gumroots we've got for supper. Or, at least, we did have loads till we started eating them…"

The stoat craned his neck and searched the woods. "Hurry

and get in the house before anything else sees you," he said, snatching up the two dead birds.

Lug hung his head, wearing the same guilty look as Dublin when he got caught digging holes in the flower beds. He held his hand out to Izzy, and they followed after the stoat.

Izzy looked around for the house he mentioned, thinking it stood behind the huge tree. But as they approached the trunk, she realized the tree *was* the house. A wide crack in the trunk ran six feet up from the ground. The stoat passed in easily, but Lug had to suck in his breath to squeeze himself inside. Dree and Izzy slipped in right behind them.

It took a moment for Izzy's eyes to adjust to the dim light. The crack opened into a large, circular room about as big as her living room back home. A fire flickered in a stone hearth in the center. The smoke wafted up through a hole in the tree trunk high above their heads. Around the edges of the room lay three pallets of dirty blankets and straw. A makeshift mobile of snail shells and acorns hung over one of the pallets, the only decoration in the house.

The stoat trotted into the center of the room and dropped his birds in the dirt beside the fire. He shook his head from side to side. With each shake, he grew taller, his arms and legs grew longer, and his face became flatter, until he was no longer a stoat, but a boy.

Another Changeling, just like Lug, just like Dree. The way the two of them had talked about their leader, Izzy had expected Selden to be an adult. But the thin boy standing in front of her couldn't be older than thirteen. He had deep-brown skin and unruly black hair that might have been curly if it weren't so filthy. Dark-brown eyes twinkled out from his dirty face.

Selden folded his arms and frowned at Lug. "You went to Hollowdell even after I told you I'd seen Unglers prowling the place?"

"I promise that I'll never—"

"And you Changed out in the open?"

Lug's eyes welled with tears. "Oh, Selden, I'm sorry! I know it was foolish of me!"

Selden sighed and shook his head. "The most annoying thing is that it's impossible to stay mad at you."

Lug rushed forward and wrapped his arms around his friend. "You know how much I hate to disappoint you!"

Selden extracted himself from the embrace. "All right, all right! Just don't do it again." He sat on a stump next to the fire, then swung his eyes to Izzy. "Now, we've got to deal with this one. Who are you and what are you doing here?"

"My name is Izzy." She walked over to him and held out her hand.

Selden crossed his arms and glared at her.

Lug took a step forward. "Izzy's traveling through on her way to the city. Going to the festival to meet her—"

Selden held out his palm. "I want *her* to say it."

Izzy gulped. "Well, it's just like Lug said…I'm going to Avhalon to meet my sister. I'm a little lost and I need…some help getting there."

Selden stared at her, unblinking. "And you're from where, exactly?"

"I am from…" Izzy's mind raced to think of a town with a fairy-sounding name. She decided it was better to be vague. "From a little village on the other side of the forest."

"Ah. The Eastern side?"

Izzy nodded slowly.

"Oh really?" asked Selden, raising his eyebrows. "You must be tired from walking then, since the Edgewood's so vast in that direction that no one knows where it ends."

Dree snickered, and Izzy felt her palms start to sweat.

Selden stood up and started to pace in a circle around her. "Or maybe you flew all this way, since it looks like you've hardly walked a mile in those shoes. Speaking of shoes." He bent down and swiped one finger across her high-tops. "I guess you stole those from somewhere? Cobblers around here don't make hideous things like that."

Izzy looked down at her feet, realizing she probably wore the least fairy-looking shoes imaginable. She held her chin up and tried her best to look composed. "I found them," she said casually. "My old shoes were all worn out from walking, and I found these lying beside the path in the woods."

"Did you?" asked Selden. He pulled out a pocketknife from his tattered trousers and flicked it open. He kept his eyes on her while he dug the dirt from under his nails with the blade tip. "What do you think, Dree? Should we believe her?"

"I don't trust her farther than I can spit," said Dree, and she spat a wad of mucus onto the dirt at her feet.

"Me neither," said Selden. He sprang at Izzy. Before she could react, he had her bent backward in a headlock.

"Let me go!" she shrieked. She grabbed his arm and tried to pull it away from her neck, her eyes on the pocketknife still in his other hand.

Selden squeezed his grip tighter. "Tell us the truth—what are you doing here?"

"Remember your manners," said Lug calmly.

Selden dropped the knife and grabbed a fistful of Izzy's hair. He pulled back, uncovering her ears.

"Ow!" she yelped.

Lug and Dree both gasped and took a step back.

"A—a human!" cried Lug.

"Yes! I'm a—human, all right?" said Izzy, struggling to choke out the words. "Now—let go—of me!"

Selden released Izzy and pushed her away from him. "I knew you didn't find those shoes," he said smugly.

Lug looked wounded. "Izzy, is it really true? After all we've been through, and you didn't even tell me?"

"Yes, it's true," Izzy said, rubbing her chafed neck. "I'm sorry I didn't tell you. I didn't know what you'd think."

"I *told* you she was a spy!" said Dree.

"Oh, will you give it a rest?" Izzy shouted. "I'm not a spy! Who in the world would I be spying on you for?"

Dree looked a little surprised to be yelled at. "Well, you could be a spy from Avhalon," she said.

Izzy threw her arms out at her side. "I don't know anything about Avhalon! But I wish I did, because maybe then I'd be able to find my sister!"

"So you are looking for your sister?" asked Lug. "Izzy, which parts of your story are true?"

"That part is true," said Izzy. "Someone called the Piper took her from the woods behind my house this morning."

As soon as she said this, Selden's smirk vanished. "Good Peter took your sister? How do you know that?"

"It's kind of a long story."

"Does it look like we have places to go?"

Izzy took a deep breath and began with Hen's disappearance. It was hard to believe it had all happened that same day. The others interrupted her with questions: How old was her sister? Did she see any other children in the woods? What exactly did the music sound like? Izzy told them everything about Netherbee Hall and Marian's true identity. When she said the word *Changeling*, Izzy noticed that Dree and Selden shifted uncomfortably. Finally, she got to the part about the cobwebs taking Marian down.

Lug lowered his head and put one hand on his chest. "One of our own Bretabairn. Poor lady."

"I could have told you to stay away from Netherbee," said Dree, lifting her nose in the air. "That place has been deserted for years. It's crawling with all sorts of wicked things."

"Well, Marian didn't know that," said Izzy. "And now it's up to me to find Hen."

Selden scratched his neck. "This is all very odd."

"Odd?" asked Izzy. "This is the worst thing that's ever happened to me in my entire life." She suddenly felt unbelievably tired. "I just want to find my sister and bring her back home."

Lug set his hand on her shoulder. "You poor little thing," he said softly. "We'll help you, Izzy. Won't we?" He looked over at his companions.

Selden snorted, and Dree spat onto the floor again.

Izzy grit her teeth. She'd been ganged up on by other kids before. Of course, those kids had been human, but otherwise, it didn't feel much different. She wished she could tell Selden and Dree to go stuff their heads in the stream. But if the rest of the Edgewood was as dangerous as Netherbee Hall or Hollowdell, she'd have to bite her tongue. As much as she hated it, she needed their help.

"Ahem," Lug said with a cough. "Selden, I haven't quite told you everything about what happened in Hollowdell. While I was trapped, we heard the Unglers. They came very close. If Izzy hadn't come along, you might never have seen me again."

"What?" cried Dree, looking horrified. "You didn't tell me they nearly caught you!"

"How did they find you?" asked Selden. "Weren't you wearing your Scarlet Stairstep?"

Lug smiled sheepishly and pointed to one of the pallets. A strand of bright-red beads lay across the dirty blanket.

Dree shook her head. "Oh, Lug, you could have been killed!"

"I'm about to kill him right now," growled Selden.

"Now, now," said Lug, his hands out in front of him. "There's no need to get upset all over again. I'm only telling you this so you'll appreciate what Izzy did for me. She's a good one, through and through."

Selden stood scratching the back of his neck. He raised one eyebrow at Izzy. "Is it true? Did you really save him?"

She nodded.

"Without a thought for her own safety," said Lug, slapping her on the back and smiling broadly. "It was a real kindness. One that deserves to be repaid."

Dree walked to Selden's side. "We are not helping this girl! Think about it. If her story is true, it means the Piper is *stealing* human children. You really want to get wrapped up in that? If we have to repay her, then let's just take her back where we found her and be done!"

"But, Dree, that wouldn't be kind at all," said Lug. "She doesn't know where she's going, and the Road's too dangerous until you get out of the Edgewood." His face suddenly brightened. "I know! Why don't we take her to the Giant's Boneyard? It's right on the border of the 'Wood. She could take up the Road from there and be on her own way."

Izzy didn't like the sound of being left in a boneyard, but it couldn't be worse than where she'd come from. She crossed her toes and hoped the others would agree to it.

Selden ran his fingers through his matted hair and sighed. "If we take her to the Boneyard, then at least we can leave her there with a clean conscience. And Lug's right—it's bad luck not to repay a favor."

Dree folded her arms. "I don't believe in luck and I haven't got a conscience. I'm not doing it."

"What are we supposed to do with her then?" asked Selden. "She's seen where we live. If we let her go and she gets caught by the Unglers, they'll make her spill her guts before they cut them out."

Izzy shuddered and wrapped her arms over her stomach.

"Please, Dree?" said Lug. "There'll be all sorts of fairies on their way to the festival. We could buy some things we need." He batted his eyelashes at her. "Maybe a new dress for you?"

"We haven't got any money, beetle brain," said Dree. Her fingers wandered down to the fraying hem of her dirty dress. "Fine. To the Boneyard, and not one step farther. But if this all ends badly, don't say I didn't warn you."

Izzy threw her arms around Lug's belly. "Oh thank you, thank you! You'll see. I won't cause you any trouble."

Selden walked past her, knocking her aside with his shoulder. He bent down and picked up the dead birds off the floor. "Dree, you build up the fire. I'll take these hedgeons outside to pluck." As he walked out the door, he threw Izzy a dirty look. "Looks like we've got another mouth to feed."

12

HEDGEONS AND PEANUT BUTTER

IZZY HADN'T REALIZED HOW hungry she was until Selden started talking about dinner. But when they all finally sat down at the wooden table to eat, her stomach grumbled its disappointment. The plucked hedgeons were no bigger than tennis balls, and there were only four gumroots left. Selden used his pocketknife to divide up the meat and hand out the portions. Izzy picked up a puny drumstick and took a bite. Either hedgeons were supposed to be pink in the center, or Selden hadn't cooked them completely.

"Oh my gosh, I nearly forgot!" She jumped up and went to the other side of the room to Hen's backpack. When she came back to the table, she held the two packages of cheese crackers and the squished peanut butter sandwiches.

"This is my contribution to dinner," she said, unwrapping the food. She gave everyone three crackers and a half a sandwich.

Dree and Selden held the crackers at arms' length, flipping them over skeptically.

Dree sniffed one and dropped it onto the table. "Ugh! Smells like paint."

"You can give yours to me if you don't want them," said Lug, licking the outsides with his black tongue. "I like the salt."

Izzy frowned. "Maybe you'll like the peanut butter better. It's the smooth kind." She waited while they all took small bites of their sandwich halves. "Well? What do you think?"

"Fnicky," mumbled Lug, his mouth full.

"What did you say?"

"I fed if *fnicky*."

"Oh!" said Izzy with a laugh. "Yeah, it's really sticky!" The sandwiches went over much better. Even Dree didn't act like she hated them.

Izzy watched them eat, chewing with their mouths open, wiping their fingers on their already dirty clothes. *One day, four Changelings.* If it wasn't happening to her, she would never believe it.

"I've read stories about you," she said. "I mean not you, specifically, but about Changelings."

Again, they all cringed when she said the word. Selden looked at the crack in the tree like someone could be listening.

Izzy lowered her voice. "That's what you are, aren't you?"

"How ever did you figure it out?" asked Dree in mock surprise. "You must be the cleverest little girl in the whole wide world."

Izzy ignored her and turned to Lug. "So what are you doing here? Shouldn't you all be pretending to be human babies or something?"

"We did," said Lug, swallowing a mouthful of peanut butter. "But we're outcasts now."

"Outcasts? What do you mean?"

"Kicked out by our human families," said Selden. He took a bite of hedgeon and pointed the bone at Lug. "This one grew too big, too fast—"

"Nearly busted my own cradle," said Lug with a smile full of crumbs.

"—and Dree could never make herself solid enough to pass as a human. Her own 'mother' tied her up in a pillowcase and"—Selden flicked his hand over his shoulder—"tossed her in a river."

"That's awful," said Izzy. She'd heard about people doing that to pets they didn't want—and that was bad enough—but never to a baby.

Dree looked up from her plate and smiled coldly. "Day before Christmas."

Izzy turned to Selden. "And what about you?"

"Selden likes to say he was cast out," said Dree. "But he ran away and came back to Faerie on his own."

"Well, I'm sure I would have been run off sooner or later," said Selden, picking his teeth with his fingernail. "Your world's got too many rules. I don't see how you can stand it."

"I guess I don't really have another option," said Izzy. She remembered what Marian told her about Grandma Jean being her only friend. If it weren't for her, maybe Marian would have run away too and come back to Faerie just like these Changelings.

"So is that why you're all so secretive?" Izzy asked. "Because you weren't supposed to come back here?"

Lug shook his head. "No, lots of Changelings end up coming back. We're—" He stopped midsentence and gulped down a big bite of food.

Izzy looked up at Dree. The girl scowled at Lug with a look that said, *Zip it*. Obviously, they weren't going to tell her too much about themselves. Not yet anyway.

"So if you switch places with human children, then you must know what happens to them," said Izzy. "Marian told me the Piper took my sister to Avhalon. Do you think that's true?"

"Oh yes," said Lug cheerfully. "Good Peter always takes human children to Avhalon. They get adopted at the Apple Festival."

"The Piper's name is *Good* Peter?" asked Izzy. "How can anyone who steals children be called *good*?"

Selden spat a piece of bone onto his plate. "It's not stealing. It's swapping."

"Not this time," Izzy corrected him. "If the Apple Festival hasn't happened yet, then that means Hen hasn't been adopted yet either. I'm going to find the Piper and tell him he's made a mistake. Hen has a family, and she needs to come home with me."

"Splendid idea," said Dree. "While you're at it, maybe you can ask him for a pony and a pretty pink carriage to ride home in."

Lug kicked her under the table. "My, my! I am stuffed, aren't you?" he said, clapping his hands together. "That was just a fantastic meal, fantastic. The hedgeons, the peanut butter, all just lovely. Eat up, Izzy. You've hardly touched a thing."

Izzy slid her plate away. "No, thank you, I'm not very hungry."

Selden pushed away from the table and stood up to stretch. "We should get to bed. We need to be off early if we're going to make any distance by nightfall tomorrow."

They all got up, leaving Izzy sitting alone with the greasy dishes.

Izzy woke up with her face plastered against a jagged piece of tree bark. Lug snored on the floor beside her. He had offered to sleep there so she could have his bed, but she wasn't sure his pallet was any cleaner than the dirt. It definitely wasn't any more comfortable. Sticks and sharp pieces of straw poked through her clothes and made her itch, and his blanket smelled like a mixture of dog hair and damp hay. She turned her head and rubbed her sore cheek. Pale morning light reached down through the opening in the top of the tree.

Izzy was just about to sit up when she heard the low murmur of voices. She turned her face and saw Selden and Dree sitting beside the hearth. She quickly shut her eyes halfway and strained to listen over the steady rumble of Lug's snores.

"Now there's no doubt," said Dree. "Peter's working for *her*. It's like I told you. He's a traitor."

Selden frowned and shook his head. "I just can't believe it. All these years. He dedicated his life to the Exchange."

"But there is no more Exchange, is there? That releases him from his obligations. Maybe this is what he wanted all along. I'm telling you, Peter was always a mystery. I never fully trusted him."

"But why would he steal a human child?"

"Because she told him to! Whatever is going on, we don't want anything to do with it. I don't know what that woman wants with a human girl, but whatever it is, she's not just going to let her go."

Selden pointed his thumb at Izzy's pallet. "That's the shrimp's problem."

"It's *our* problem if the shrimp gets picked up and questioned, which is sure to happen once she gets to Avhalon."

Selden snorted. "If she even makes it that far. She has no idea what she's getting into. Are humans really this dumb?"

"Apparently, which is why we should stay away from them." Dree leaned in close to Selden and raised one eyebrow. "I know why you want to take her to the Boneyard, and it's got nothing to do with repaying a good deed. You want to see if we can find anyone going to the festival who has some news."

He shrugged away from her. "So what if I do? Don't *you*? Sometimes I think you've stopped caring…"

"Don't be stupid. Of course I care. But what can we do about it? Just the three of us? For now, the only thing we can do is keep ourselves hidden."

Selden slumped and looked down at the ground. "We've been hiding for so long. I just want to know what happened to them, that's all."

Dree reached out to put her hand on his arm, but then pulled it back as he turned away. She watched him for a moment, a sad look on her face. Then she got up and went outside.

Izzy shut her eyes tight. She tried to piece together what she had just heard. Who was this woman they were talking about? She had something to do with the Piper and with Hen. Whatever it was, getting Hen back home was going to be more difficult than Izzy had thought. Selden's words burned in her ears: *She has no idea what she's getting into.* Izzy was used to other kids talking about her behind her back, but this was different. What Selden said stung so badly because Izzy knew it was true.

A hot tear ran down, soaking the hair at her temple. What *had* she gotten herself into? Maybe Marian could have rescued Hen, but Izzy didn't stand a chance, not on her own. She couldn't even get out of this stupid forest by herself. All she wanted was to open her eyes and find out that none of this had ever happened, to close the book and end the story.

Izzy heard Selden's boots shuffling closer across the dirt

floor. She blinked away her tears. Before he had a chance to say anything, she bolted up and pretended to rub the sleep out of her eyes.

"Oh, you're up," he said. "Now we've just got to wake the sleeping bear." He leaned over Lug and shook his shoulder. "Hey, snoring beauty! Come on, time to get up."

"What's for breakfast?" mumbled Lug.

"Whatever we can scrounge up on the Road," said Dree. She tossed a strand of crimson beads onto Lug's chest.

Lug sat up and looped the necklace over his head.

"What is that?" Izzy asked.

"Scarlet Stairstep." Lug held up the necklace so she could see. The beads were chunks of the shelflike mushrooms that grew on the outside of Yawning Top, strung together on a piece of twine. "So the Unglers can't pick up our scent."

Izzy didn't think anything could mask Lug's scent, but one whiff of the musky fungus proved her wrong. She now realized what had smelled so terrible outside Yawning Top. The mushrooms reeked like a pile of dirty, mildewed socks.

"Whoa, yeah." She coughed. "That's strong."

"Here," said Dree, throwing her a smaller strand. "You should wear one too, since you slept in Lug's bed."

"Lucky me," said Izzy, holding the necklace away from her.

"Let's go already," snapped Selden. "Now are you gonna get up and put your shoes on, or do we have to do everything for you?"

Izzy threw him a hateful look. She wanted to ask, *What's the point? It's all hopeless, isn't it?* But instead, she put on the foul necklace, slipped on her sneakers, and followed the others outside.

THE VERY HELPFUL BROWNIE

THEY WALKED ALL DAY, following the creek, never stopping unless it was to listen for the Unglers. At times, Izzy wondered if they'd gone in the wrong direction and were actually headed east into that vast, never-ending part of the forest that Selden had mentioned. She was so anxious to get to Hen that her stomach was in a permanent knot. Or that could have been the rancid mushrooms strung around her neck.

Izzy couldn't exactly prod the others to go faster, since she was the slowest one. Even when the Changelings were in their child forms, they hiked too fast for her to keep up. The thorns that scratched her arms and legs didn't seem to bother them. And the rocky ground didn't slow them down, even though Selden was the only one who wore shoes. By the time he barked at Izzy to ride on Lug's shoulders, she was grateful for the rest. To distract herself from thinking about Hen, she watched the Changelings. Selden and Dree were snobs, but they were the most fascinating snobs Izzy had ever met.

Selden jogged ahead, scouting out the way as a lean, black wolf or a stag with a rack of velvety black antlers. Sometimes, he'd disappear for a long time, then rejoin them as the stoat, holding a fat bird egg in his mouth. Dree either zipped along in her butterfly form or darted through the treetops as a silvery, scissor-tailed bird.

The next time Izzy and Lug were out of earshot of the others, she leaned down and whispered in his ear. "Why doesn't Selden turn into a bird too? Flying seems a lot easier than walking."

"Selden can't do birds," Lug answered. "He's *Sharp points against the world*, you see."

"He's what?"

"Every Changeling has a range of things they can be. There's an old book of poetry in Avhalon called *The Bretabairn*. That's an old-timey name for Changelings. Each poem in the book lists the different creatures a Changeling might specialize in. The poem that fits Selden best ends with the line, *Sharp points against the world*. I think it suits him pretty well, don't you?"

"A stoat, a wolf, a stag. Yeah, I guess it does."

"Now, take Dree. What do you think her poem would say?"

Izzy watched the gray bird swooping gracefully through the branches. "Well, the animals she Changes into are so delicate. Which is weird, because her personality reminds me most of a snapping turtle."

"Ha! You've got it!" Lug said with a laugh. "She's *Fierceness beneath the lace wing*. Are you sure you haven't read the book yourself?"

Izzy smiled. "And what about you? What does your poem say?"

"Mine is quite fitting. I've never been able to Change into anything small. It ends with *Stout body for a strong heart*."

"I think that's perfect for you," said Izzy, patting the top of his hairy head. "But wait a minute—you Changed into a human baby once, didn't you? That's pretty small."

"That's different. I never *Changed* into a baby. I just put on its Likeness."

Izzy sighed. "You've lost me again."

"When I become a bear or a ram or any of those creatures from my poem, that's a true Change. Taking on those forms comes naturally, just like breathing. I could be those animals for days and never get tired. But I can also put on the Likeness of something that isn't in my poem."

Izzy thought of her first meeting with Lug. "Like a mossy boulder?"

"Exactly! I'm good at that one. A Likeness is just pretend. I have to concentrate to hold on to it."

"And you couldn't hold on to a little baby's form."

Lug chuckled. "Can you imagine me in a diaper? I tried to

tell Good Peter I wasn't up for it, but when the Piper says it's your turn for the Exchange, you go. Didn't work out so well for me. But if a Changeling ends up in the right home and it's a good fit, they usually stay. They wear their human Likeness so long it becomes a second skin, and they get stuck that way."

Izzy nodded, thinking of Marian and how the old woman could only Change the shape of her ears. She still didn't know what to think about the Exchange. Stealing babies seemed cruel, even if the parents did get a Changeling in return. She started to ask Lug about it but stopped herself. He seemed so proud to be a part of it, and she didn't want to hurt his feelings. Marian had said it was complicated. It must be if someone as sweet as Lug was involved.

They slept in the open that night without a fire, while the Changelings took turns at the watch. Lug showed Izzy how to heap dried leaves over herself to block out the chilly night air. She didn't think anything could be less comfortable than his bed of sticks, but this proved her wrong. She itched like crazy from the scratchy leaves, and every time she moved even a millimeter, her pile would collapse and expose her to the cold. So she lay as still as possible, trying not to think about all the bad things that might have happened to her sister.

If she fell asleep at all that night, it wasn't for more than a few minutes at a time. In the middle of one of her dozes, she felt the toe of someone's boot nudging her in the side. She sprung up to see Selden standing over her.

"Is it morning yet?" she mumbled hopefully.

"Almost. Did you have a good night's sleep?"

"Oh absolutely," she answered without much conviction. She shook the dirty leaves from her hair. "I just love sleeping outdoors. It's so relaxing."

"Really? You look like you've been trampled on by an ogre. You'll be glad to know we're almost there."

"We're almost to the Giant's Boneyard?"

"No, we're almost to Shank's. Come on."

Izzy grabbed her backpack and followed after him. "What's Shank's?"

"A trading post. You can't go to the city dressed like a human, or you'll draw too much attention to yourself. And you'll need a hat to cover those ridiculous things." He pointed to her ears. "Shank trades in goods from Faerie and Earth. He'll have something decent for you to wear, and hopefully he'll take those clown clothes from you in exchange. He's a brownie."

Izzy brightened at the familiar word. "A brownie! Like from the tale about the shoemaker."

Selden raised his eyebrows. "I haven't heard that one."

"You know, the old shoemaker can't make all his shoes, so the brownies come to his house in the night and make them for him. They don't take any of the credit; they just want to help."

Selden turned with a wry smile. "Oh yes, old Shank is real helpful. He'll help you right out of the shirt on your back."

An hour later, they crossed a rocky ravine and arrived at a low, wood cabin with a porch on the front. A sign with peeling paint read *Winchester Shank's Fine Apparel and Wares. Buy, sell, trade.*

Selden whispered instructions to the others. "Everyone stick to your normal forms. No Changing until we're out of sight from here. Shank doesn't know what we are, and I want to keep it that way."

"What about me?" asked Izzy. "Won't he say something about the way I'm dressed?"

"Just keep your ears hidden and leave all the talking to me," said Selden. "And whatever you do, don't go blabbing that nonsense about the shoemaker!"

Lug stayed outside to keep watch, while the others walked up the porch steps. Izzy smoothed her hair down over her ears and followed Dree and Selden to the front door. Selden leaned against it and knocked loudly. They heard shuffling feet across a sawdust floor. A round hatch in the door swung aside, and a beady, bloodshot eye peered out at them. The eye swiveled around and landed on Selden. The hatch swung shut again.

Selden knocked harder.

"We're closed!" said a scratchy voice from inside.

"You are not closed, Shank! Now let us in! We've got wares to trade."

"Ha! Whatever you got, Selden, I don't want it. You ain't

brought in anything worth a dung ball in over a year, and I ain't got time to fool around with your handmade junk."

"It's not me that's here to trade," Selden shouted at the door. "It's my friend. She's just come back from a little trip, and she has some things I think you'll be interested in. So let us in!"

After a pause, the circular hatch swung back halfway, and the beady eye reappeared. Selden grabbed Izzy by the arm and pulled her in front of the door so the eye could see her. It looked her up and down, then disappeared. She heard the sounds of keys being turned and bolts sliding, then the door swung open.

The man behind it stood about even with Izzy's shoulder. He wore a brown waistcoat and a pinched, sour look on his face. He worked his mouth and spat out a slug of something oily and brown into a tin cup. "I might be amenable to talkin' to her," he said. "The rest of you can wait outside."

Selden shouldered his way past the little man and walked into the cabin. "And let you swindle her out of everything she's got? We'll all come in, thank you. You brownies are so kind." He threw Izzy a smug grin.

Inside, they walked up to a long wooden counter. Behind it, the walls were lined with shelves full of shoes—boots, slippers, fancy dress pumps, sandals—most of them looking very old fashioned. The cabin held other items as well. A section of one of the walls was devoted to hats hanging on pegs, and a glass-fronted counter displayed music boxes, jewelry, and other trinkets. Dree walked directly over to a rack of clothes in the corner.

The little man bent down on one knee to examine Izzy's high-tops. "Interestin'," he said. "Where'd you come by these?"

Selden stood with one elbow leaning against the counter. "She just got back from a trip to Earth. Stealing chickens off a farm in Chitterhaw. Didn't you, Izzy?"

She nodded and squared her shoulders back, trying to give off the air of a chicken thief.

"I see," said Shank. "You got a good eye, girlie, a good eye. I ain't seen this type before. Course I ain't seen much of anything in a good while. These days, you cain't find a human that even believes in fairies, much less wants to trade with 'em. Most of the paths into Earth are closed up or lost, and the open ones got Unglers prowlin' around 'em. Business has nearly dried right up."

Shank stood up with a groan and put his hands on his hips. He gave Izzy a greasy smile. "Tell you what, girlie. I'll offer you a pair of real nice slippers—"

"Oh no, you don't," interrupted Selden. "She wants boots. You can keep the ratty slippers for yourself."

Shank scowled at him. "Fine," he said, shuffling behind his counter. "You want boots, you can have 'em. But my selection ain't what it used to be." He climbed up on a rolling ladder attached to the shelves. "You want human-made or fairy-made?"

"Does she look like she wants a pair that'll wear out in two days?" scoffed Selden. "Fairy-made, of course."

Shank rolled himself to the boot section, then rolled back toward them with his arms full of boots. He dumped them on the counter in front of them.

Selden began picking through them, turning each one over to examine their soles. "Nope… Not this one either. Too stiff…"

"What about these?" asked Izzy, holding up a pair of black riding boots.

"Nope. They've got laces, and laces break," said Selden, clearly basking in his superior boot knowledge. Finally, he picked up a light-brown pair of men's boots with buckles on the side and flexed the soles back and forth. "These. They'll last the longest, and they're already broken in."

Izzy looked at them skeptically. "But they're humongous. They'll never fit me."

Shank snapped his fingers and shuffled out through a door behind the counter. "Ain't a problem," he called from the back. In a moment, he emerged with his hands in thick mitts, struggling to carry a heavy black pot emitting ribbons of steam. He set the pot down in front of a chair in the center of the room. "All right, girlie. Boots in."

Izzy took the boots from the counter and started to lower them into the steaming pot.

"What do you think you're doin'!" cried Shank, rushing

over to her. "You gotta put 'em on your feet first, you ninny! How else will you know when they're the right size?"

Izzy looked down at the rising steam. "You've got to be joking."

"Don't be a baby," said Selden. "It doesn't hurt. Shank shrunk my own boots for me, and see how well they fit?"

"Back when you had somethin' worth tradin'," Shank said with a sneer. He took Izzy by the hand and led her to the chair. "Take a seat, girlie. There you go. Now, you just remove them lovely shoes, and we'll get your new boots all shrunk up perfect."

"I hope you all know what you're doing," said Izzy, removing her high-tops. She pulled on the big boots and swung her feet over the lip of the black pot. Gripping the edge of the chair, she lowered them in slowly.

"All at once!" ordered Shank. "Or else the toes'll shrink different from the rest of 'em."

Izzy held her breath and let her feet fall into the pot. Hot liquid seeped in through the top of the boots and surrounded her toes as it bubbled. Amazingly, she didn't feel her skin scalding.

"That's it. Now, when you feel 'em start to get snug, pull 'em out."

After a moment, she felt the squeak of leather around her ankles, and she yanked her feet out of the pot. The boots fit her perfectly.

"What'd I tell ya?" shouted Shank, slapping his leg. "Have a walk around, and make sure they're right. No refunds once you walk out the door."

Izzy stood up and strode around the room. The leather was soft and buttery, and the buckles made a satisfying little clinking sound when she stepped. The best part was that the heels gave her at least a half inch of added height.

"There you go, Izzy. Your first decent pair of shoes," said Selden. He leaned back against the counter casually. "So, Shank. Hear any news from town lately?"

The brownie turned Izzy's old shoes over in his hands, looking at the soles. "Apple Festival starts in a couple days. They say *she* is gonna grace everyone with her royal presence."

"Oh really?" asked Selden. "The queen?"

Shank spat into his cup. "Ha! If she's the queen, then I'm Father Time." He looked over his shoulder like someone might be listening at the door. "Should be a real spectacle," he said more quietly. "She don't usually leave that castle she built for herself. Likes to send her little pets out to do her nasty work instead."

Selden stared at the floor, scratching his nose. "Interesting… very interesting."

Dree coughed. "A-*hem.*"

Selden snapped his head up. "Well, Shank, it's been lovely, but we should get moving. Izzy needs clothes as well. I'll leave you two to sort that out. Maybe you can find some baby elf pajamas small enough to fit her."

Izzy rolled her eyes at him.

Shank grumbled something under his breath as Selden

exited, then turned to Izzy again. "I'll get ya all set up, girlie," he said, leading her to the clothes rack. "Got some pixie clothes that might be your size—hey! Get your filthy paws away from those dresses!" He scuttled over to Dree, who had been admiring a white lace dress. He swatted her hand away. "Those are expensive, much too good for you. Just look at your fingernails," he said nastily. "Get on out of here before you stain everythin'!"

Dree's cheeks flushed pale pink, and she hid her hands behind her back.

Shank leaned close to Izzy. "Hope she didn't dirty up anythin' you're interested in," he whispered loudly. "Every time she comes in here, she tries to talk me into a new dress, but that bag o' bones never has anythin' worth tradin'. I don't run a charity operation, you know."

Izzy watched as Dree stalked to the front of the store with her chin held high. She recognized the look on Dree's face. It was the look of someone who doesn't want to give a bully the satisfaction of seeing them cry.

Izzy tried to block out Shank's groveling while she looked through the clothes for something that would fit her. Before long, she found a light-blue button-down shirt she could wear over her T-shirt, a navy jacket with a hood to replace her striped sweatshirt, and brown trousers to replace the jeans.

She gave Shank her leather belt in exchange for a hat from his collection. It was made from oiled canvas with a wide brim and a leather strap that cinched under her chin. Izzy changed into her new clothes behind a little screen, making sure to tuck the Scarlet Stairstep necklace under her new shirt. When she picked up her old clothes, something fell out of her jeans pocket and thudded onto the floor.

Izzy bent down to pick it up. It was the tiny blue bottle that she'd shoved into her pocket back at Netherbee Hall. She'd forgotten all about it until just now. She read the label again: *Root Revive*, written in scrawling cursive.

"Oh, Marian, I wish you were with me now!" Izzy whispered. She squeezed the bottle in her palm and tucked it in the inside pocket of her new jacket.

She stepped out from behind the screen, handed Shank her old clothes, and walked in front of the mirror. She almost laughed out loud at how ridiculous she looked, like someone who actually would steal chickens for a living.

Shank stood behind his counter, going through Izzy's old clothes and scribbling notes in a record book. "Come on up, and I'll get ya a receipt, unless you got somethin' else you wanna trade."

Izzy's eyes drifted to the white lace dress on the clothes rack. She wondered how long it had been since Dree had a new dress. From the looks of it, her current one would disintegrate to threads before long. But Izzy didn't think what she had left to trade would be enough for the lace. Then she got an idea.

She set Hen's backpack on the counter and started feeling around inside.

Hen had packed all sorts of junk: a plastic tiara, some crayons, a kaleidoscope. Finally, Izzy's fingers landed on a plastic snow globe souvenir from their trip to the beach last summer. She flicked the snow globe so that it rolled out onto the counter toward the brownie.

"Oh dear!" she said, reaching for it. "Can you hand that to me, please?"

Shank picked it up and turned it over curiously. The white flecks of fake snow fluttered down onto a little plaster dolphin, poised in midleap. "That's an interestin' little trinket you got there."

"Please handle that more carefully!" she chided him. "It's *very* valuable."

"Is it?" Shank held it up and read the words on the bottom. "Fort. Walton. Beach. That a human town?"

"Oh yes. One of the greatest cities on Earth."

Shank looked impressed.

"It's the capital of the United States," she continued. "The president lives there."

"Abraham Lincoln?" whispered the brownie.

"Mmm-hmm," said Izzy, nodding importantly. "The dolphin is his special symbol. It represents…um…honesty."

Shank clutched the snow globe in the crook of his arm. "Say, what would you trade for this here?"

Izzy put one hand to her chest. "Oh, I couldn't *possibly* let you have it. It's such an important treasure."

"Come on now," said Shank. "Everyone's got their price."

She swept her eyes around the room to the rack of clothes. "Well, I guess I might be able to think of something."

Izzy marched down the porch steps. She wanted to make the buckles on her new boots clink.

"Say, will you look at that!" said Lug, staring at her new getup. "That can't be the same girl I met back in Hollowdell, can it? You look like a real fairy farm girl in those clothes!"

"At least you don't look like a circus clown anymore," said Selden. "But you took your sweet time in there, didn't you?"

"Mr. Shank drives a hard bargain," said Izzy. "Actually, I think he did cheat me. Somehow, he talked me into giving him my whole backpack for this." She pulled the white dress out from behind her back. "I don't know why I agreed to it. I can't stand to wear dresses."

"You got swindled all right," said Selden, turning his nose up at the dress. "Now, if the fashion show is over, can we finally get a move on?"

Lug followed after Selden, then turned back to Izzy and nodded at the dress in her hands. "You might give that to Dree if you don't want it. She loves dresses."

Dree hadn't taken her eyes off it. Izzy held it out to her

nonchalantly. She thought Dree might reject it if she made it into too big a deal.

Dree held out her glassy hand and took the dress. "Thank you," she whispered.

"Oh, it's nothing really."

Dree stared back with her soft, gray eyes. "It's something to me." Then she turned on her heel and dashed after the others, a ghostly blur moving through the trees.

THE OLDEST TRICK

By MIDDAY, EVEN THE Changelings were dragging from the heat. They hadn't seen or heard any signs of the Unglers during their whole trip, so Selden eased up on the grueling pace and agreed they could take turns dipping in the creek. The stony stream they'd been following had grown wider and deeper, until it was more like a river. They now had to climb down a steep bank to reach the swift-moving water.

Izzy took the last turn. She stood barefoot in the cool shallows, tossing sticks out into the current and thinking about her sister.

The last time she and Hen had gone swimming, Hen had done a cannonball and soaked Izzy's journal. Izzy had been so mad she couldn't even speak. But that night, Hen made Izzy a new one out of stapled sheets of construction paper and slipped it under her pillow. That's how it always was—Hen bungled things, and Izzy eventually forgave her. Not this time.

Now Izzy was the one who'd made a mess of everything, and Hen was nowhere to apologize to.

A voice from above jolted her out of her thoughts. "Come on, Izzy! You're slower than slithermold!" Dree, wearing the new lace dress, stood above on the rocky bank. She grinned down at Izzy playfully. "Last one to catch up to Lug has to smell his pits!"

"No fair! You can fly!" shouted Izzy, wading out of the water. She put on her socks and boots and then climbed up the steep bank to follow Dree. She ran after her for a few steps, then remembered something. "Just a second!" she called out, turning around. "I forgot my necklace!"

Izzy climbed back down to the creek where she had left her Scarlet Stairstep hanging. As she reached for it, she saw motion in the corner of her eye. She turned around and stifled a scream.

She stood two steps away from an exact replica of herself. Not a mirror. A flesh and blood, real-life Izzy.

She blinked her eyes. She opened her mouth to call out for Dree, but the replica put one finger to its lips. It smiled at her.

Izzy was mesmerized. "What—what are you?"

The replica said nothing. Izzy's own hazel eyes stared back at her from beneath her own dark eyebrows. Her clone hooked its thumbs together and fluttered its fingers in the air.

"Bird? Are you trying to say something about a bird?" asked Izzy.

It smiled and nodded, then pointed to the top of its head.

"Crown? Head? Brain?"

Another nod. The clone pointed at Izzy and then did all the hand signs together.

Izzy scrunched up her eyebrows, trying to understand. "Bird…brain…me. Me, bird, brain?"

Her double began to snicker. Spit flew out of its mouth as it folded over in hysterics, clutching at its side. "Your face! You should see your face!" it shrieked between fits of laughter.

Izzy's cheeks burned. She knew that voice. She shoved her double in the shoulder and stomped past it. Only it didn't look like her anymore. It had Changed back into what it really was.

Selden.

"I can't believe you actually fell for that!" he said, laughing as he climbed up the bank after her. "Don't you know that's the oldest Changeling prank there is?"

Izzy marched on, fuming.

"Oof, I think I sprained something squeezing myself down into your wormy little Likeness," he said, rubbing his shoulder.

Izzy spun around and kicked her boot at his shin.

He dodged it easily. "Hey, what's that all about?"

"I am *sick* of you making fun of me! Why can't you just leave me alone?"

"Hey, hey, come on," said Selden. "You've got to admit that was hilarious. You humans are too serious!"

Izzy turned away and started walking. "Oh, I know. According to you, we're too serious, too slow, too spoiled, too dumb—"

"Yes, you're finally catching on!"

"If we're so awful, then why go to Earth and switch places with one of us?"

Selden jogged along beside her. "When you're a Changeling, the Exchange is what you do. It's been going on for a thousand years. More, maybe. Ever since our worlds split off from each other."

Izzy started to ask him what he meant but stopped herself. She was not about to give him the satisfaction of teaching her something. In fact, she was determined to act like she wasn't interested in him at all.

Mischief flickered in Selden's eyes. "Oh, don't tell me you don't know what I'm talking about. In all those storybooks of yours, you never read about our worlds separating?"

Izzy clenched her fists and kept walking.

"I could tell you all about it," he said in a singsong voice. "If you ask nicely."

"Go jump in a bog," she grumbled. But she only made it a few more steps before her curiosity overcame her pride. Izzy had read every fairy tale she could get her hands on, but she'd never heard of Faerie and Earth separating. She stopped and folded her arms. "Fine. I don't know what you're talking about. Will you please tell me?"

Selden waved his hand. "Well, the truth is, I don't really know much about the whole thing…"

"Oh, you are so *annoying!*" she shouted, running away from him.

He laughed and caught up to her. "All right, all right! I do know that fairies and humans used to live together in the same world. But they never could get along, so one day, they decided to split up. They were never meant to be completely separated though. Everyone assumed there would always be fairies and humans going back and forth between the two worlds."

He continued, walking backward, with his hands in his pockets. "But then humans stopped coming here. Then they stopped believing in Faerie at all. And that's when Good Peter decided that every now and then, some humans would get swapped for fairies and vice versa. That's where we come in."

Izzy rolled her eyes. "Aren't you important?"

"Yes, actually, we are. These days, the Exchange is the only thing keeping our worlds connected."

She raised an eyebrow. "If you're so high and mighty, then why don't you live in some grand castle or something? Instead of hiding out like a bunch of scared criminals?"

Selden's grin disappeared. He winced, like he'd been stung. "You really want to know? It's because—" He paused and looked past Izzy, into the trees.

"Well? Because why?"

"Shhh!" Selden stood frozen, one finger to his lips.

A high-pitched squeal echoed in the distance.

Dree and Lug came crashing back through the brush, their faces tense with fear.

"Coming…through the trees!" said Dree, panting. "Unglers!"

THE UNGLERS

SELDEN LOOKED OVER DREE'S shoulder. "How many?"

She held up two fingers.

"Did they hear you?"

"I don't know. But they're close and coming this way. We have to get out of here!"

Selden surveyed the dense bushes surrounding them. "We'll make too much noise if we try to run now. We can't let them know we're here. We need to hide!"

Dree took off her Scarlet Stairstep and tossed it at Lug. "Here, take mine!" In a flash of silver, she transformed into a bird and shot up into the forest canopy.

"Oh, why can't I do that?" whimpered Lug, draping the extra necklace over his head.

"Sit right there and be quiet," said Selden, pointing to the base of a nearby tree. "They can't find you if they can't smell you."

Lug huddled next to the tree and hugged his knees. He drew his head down between his shoulders. His skin grew mottled and patchy until he looked just like the moss-covered stone Izzy had seen on the path. He shut his eyes, and all trace of his face vanished.

More shrieks pierced the stillness, closer this time.

Selden grabbed Izzy's hand and pulled her toward the trunk of a large magnolia tree. "Climb up! Hurry!"

He laced his fingers together and bent down. Izzy placed her boot into his hands, and he shoved her up into the lower branches of the tree. She managed to climb a little farther on her own, but the higher branches were just out of reach. Selden Changed into the stoat and scampered up into a nearby pine. He coiled himself around a branch, his little black ears twitching back and forth.

Izzy hugged the tree trunk and strained to listen over the gurgling noises of the creek behind her. She peered down through gaps between the dark magnolia leaves. Slow, tense minutes went by. Then something rustled in the leaf litter below, shuffling closer. Izzy held her breath.

She saw their hands first. Long fingers, gray and gnarled like dead twigs, felt their way forward, groping constantly over the forest floor as if they had eyes at their tips. Their arms were stringy, nothing but gray skin and coarse hair stretched over bones. They lumbered slowly into full view, their backs hunched over like old men. But these beasts could never be mistaken for men. They swung heavy, tusked heads side to side, sniffing the air with hoglike snouts.

The two Unglers worked their way toward Lug until they stood directly in front of him. One rose up on its back legs and lifted its head to sniff the face of the boulder. Folds of warty skin covered the sockets where its eyes should have been.

Izzy bit down on her lower lip. If Lug lost his concentration, he might let go of the Likeness of the boulder. She had to help him. She reached for a magnolia cone and twisted it until it snapped free from its branch. She tossed the dried cone away from Lug, where it thudded onto the ground.

The Unglers wheeled around in the direction of the sound. But instead of following after the cone, one of the Unglers dropped to the ground at Lug's feet and rooted in the dirt. He jerked his head up and gave two wet snorts. The other one joined him. They snorted back and forth at each other, then began creeping toward the magnolia.

Izzy held her breath, waiting for them to keep moving on. But the Unglers didn't leave. They circled the magnolia slowly. Izzy reached her fingers up to her neck. She felt for the Scarlet Stairstep that Lug had given her, but her neck was bare. Her stomach dropped. She'd left it hanging from the branch beside the creek.

Directly below her, the Unglers pressed their snouts against the magnolia, leaving dark, slimy trails along the trunk. The wheezing snorts grew faster and heavier. Izzy cringed at the disgusting sound and rose up on her toes. She had thought she was high enough off the ground, but now she realized the Unglers might be able to reach her with their long arms.

She grabbed a branch overhead, holding onto it for balance as she carefully inched out farther along the tree limb. If she could only get farther away from the trunk, she could reach a smaller branch and pull herself higher up into the tree. She glanced at Selden. He shook his head at her and mouthed the words, *Be still.*

Suddenly, an Ungler shot its arm straight up at Izzy, grazing the heel of her boot with its fingers. She kicked her foot away and scooted faster out onto the limb.

"No, Izzy! Stop!" Selden hissed from his perch in the pine.

Izzy couldn't breathe. Could they climb trees with those hands? No longer worried about being quiet, she scooted out along the branch. The Ungler beneath her groped for her legs while the other stood at the base of the tree, squealing shrilly. Above her, she saw another, thicker branch. Izzy reached for it. Six more inches and she could make it. She stood on her toes…

Crack! The branch beneath her snapped. Izzy crashed onto the ground. The two Unglers spun around. Their wet nostrils flared in and out as they stepped slowly toward her. Izzy struggled to her feet.

"Be still!" Selden called. He Changed back into a boy and clapped his hands. "Hey, hey, look up here!" he shouted.

The Unglers didn't turn at the sound of his voice. They felt the air around Izzy's head, their leathery fingertips wriggling like thick worms. Izzy stood still, her heart pumping so hard she could hear it.

"Hold on, Izzy," said Selden, climbing down. "Don't run—"

Their fingers hovered inches from her face.

Izzy turned and fled. Her hat fell behind her, catching on the cord around her neck. The Unglers were close behind, loping through the woods with their hands on the ground like apes.

Izzy screamed and ran faster. She heard the sound of rushing water as the steep bank of the creek appeared suddenly in front of her. Before she could climb down, she felt hands on her back. She threw herself onto the ground and covered her face. The Unglers scrabbled over her, clawing at her neck and arms, trying to turn her over. Saliva dripped onto her, rolling down her collar.

Izzy grasped at the ground until her fingers found a stick. She rolled over, face-to-face with one of the beasts. She jabbed the stick as hard as she could into the place where its eye should have been. The creature squealed and recoiled. It held the side of its face and backed away.

She heard a growl, then snarling and gnashing teeth, and suddenly, the other Ungler was off her as well. Izzy jumped to her feet. The Ungler Izzy had stabbed writhed on the ground a few yards away. A black wolf had its jaws clamped around the other's shoulder, pulling it down to its knees. The monster reached up and clawed at the wolf's face. Selden yelped and let go. He backed up, hackles raised, until he stood in front of Izzy.

The Ungler stood before them, its hunched back heaving up and down. Its companion got to its feet, still clutching its bleeding eye socket. Both swayed their heads as they advanced toward Selden and Izzy. The Unglers looked straight at them like they could see. The closest one charged forward.

Wham! Something massive and brown slammed into it. The monster shrieked as it fell over the edge of the steep bank, splashing into the water below. It flailed its long arms, grasping for something to hold, but the swift current dragged it into deep water and away downstream.

The Ungler Izzy had stabbed stood swaying on its back legs, turning its wounded head back and forth. It snarled, bared its teeth, then turned and ran. It galloped away on all fours, its squeals fading behind it.

Izzy exhaled, relieved. Beside her, a shaggy bear lay on the ground, covering his head with both arms. Lug's whole body shook as he Changed back to himself. Selden, also back in his boy form, pressed his fingers to the scratch on his cheek.

Izzy wanted to thank him for saving her life, but she could barely get the words out. "Selden—I—"

"What are you doing without your Scarlet Stairstep?" he shouted. "I'm sure you're covered in Lug's smell. You nearly got us all killed!"

Izzy pointed upstream. "I went back to get it, but then *someone* thought it would be funny to play a trick on me!"

"Oh, so now it's my fault? I should've let them rip you to shreds!"

A bird swooped down and landed at their feet, transforming back into Dree. "Shut up, both of you! Who cares whose fault it is? The real question is, how did they find us?"

They all went quiet.

"I thought you said they stay near the Road," said Izzy.

"They do. Or at least they did," said Selden. "We've never seen them this far from it before. Dree, did you see where that one went?"

She nodded. "Back in the direction we came from. He's probably gone to get reinforcements."

Lug groaned. Izzy helped him stand up and held on to his trembling hands.

Selden rubbed his cheek. The blood already had begun to dry. "I don't know if we could handle more than two of them."

"Absolutely not," whimpered Lug.

"Let's cross the creek here," said Selden. "It'll help mask our scent. We'll bushwhack straight for the Boneyard."

They backtracked to the spot where Izzy left her necklace. The mud all around had been kicked up and trampled. As they were leaving, something on the ground caught Izzy's eye. She bent down and picked it up. It was a cluster of broken snail shells and acorns strung together with a piece of twine.

"That's from our mobile!" cried Lug, reaching out for the shells. "The one I made for Dree's birthday!"

Dree's hands flew to her mouth. "Do you know what this means?"

No one answered, but everyone knew. The Unglers had found Yawning Top. Izzy could see the fear spread over each of the Changelings' faces as they realized their home was no longer the safe haven it once had been. Without a word, Selden turned and motioned for the others to follow him. Lug let the cracked shells fall out of his hand and stepped on them, grinding them into the mud.

A TRUCE

Moonlight filtered down through the trees by the time they reached the Giant's Boneyard. Here, the Edgewood thinned out to make room for large sandstone boulders, just like the ones in Izzy's yard back home. The stones gleamed white in the moonlight, forming the shape of a colossal skeleton half-buried in the ground. If they truly were the bones of a long-dead giant, he would have stretched the length of a house. Selden led the way to the tallest boulder, the skeleton's shoulder, and they all climbed to the top of it.

"This is good," he said, scanning their surroundings. "We'll be able to see anything coming before it gets to us. I'll take the first watch."

He Changed into a wolf and sat down on the stone, his ears pointed at the trees. Dree Changed into a white cat striped with silver. She sat beside him, and they began whispering to each other, too low for Izzy to hear. She followed Lug over the boulders until they reached the giant's skull.

Lug curled up in a hollow depression that resembled an eye socket. He patted the rock. "Come on. Rest here with me," he said to Izzy.

She sat down beside him and hugged her knees to her chest. "There's no way I can sleep. What if those things find us again?"

"I've never been so close to an Ungler before," said Lug with a shudder. "When they put those nasty fingers all over my face, I felt like fainting."

"But you were so brave, the way you charged into them like that. All I could do was run."

"When I saw them about to hurt you and Selden, something snapped in me. We got lucky there were only two. The Unglers usually prowl the woods with triple that number."

Izzy looked over her shoulder at Dree and Selden. "You guys can't go back to Yawning Top now, can you? What are you going to do?"

"I don't know," he said with a sigh. "But I suppose that's what those two are talking about right now. A terrible shame. I really loved that tree. Almost felt like a proper home."

Home. The word sent a pang of longing right through Izzy's chest. If she were home right now, she'd be sitting at the kitchen table reading stories to Hen, while her parents did the dishes. Comfortable. Safe. Izzy shut her eyes to make the thought go away.

"Lug, do you have a mom and dad? I don't mean the human family you lived with. I mean a real mother and father."

"No, I'm an orphan." Lug pointed to where Selden and Dree sat talking. "All Changelings are."

Izzy felt guilty for asking. "Oh. I'm sorry."

Lug yawned and patted her knee. "Don't be sorry. Good Peter travels around Faerie, rounding us all up. We grow up together, take care of each other. Then, before you know it, it's your turn to do the Exchange."

"I still don't understand the Exchange," said Izzy. "Why do you do it?"

"Well, without the Exchange, Faerie and Earth would be completely cut off from one another. Even though our worlds split up, they still need each other. Without fairies, Earth would be a dreary place with no magic at all. And Faerie needs humans for…well, it needs them for…" Lug chuckled. "I guess I don't remember why! But there is a reason. Selden must be rubbing off on me. He's a little harsh on humans."

"Just a little," said Izzy. "But what I meant was: why do *you* do the Exchange? Why leave a magic place like Faerie for boring old Earth?" Izzy glanced at Selden and lowered her voice. "Don't tell him I said that, or he'll never quit gloating."

Lug smiled, and his eyes disappeared behind his downy cheeks. "Selden likes to brag about how much better Faerie is than Earth, but he did the Exchange for the same reason as all the rest of us. To get the chance to have a family." Lug yawned again and shut his eyes. "Course we're our own little family now. But that's just what friends do, don't they?"

Izzy turned her face away from his. "I kind of wouldn't know," she said softly. "Can I tell you something, Lug? I think you might be my very first one."

A deep snore rumbled beside her. Izzy looked at Lug's sleeping face and smiled. Then she curled up beside him and shut her eyes.

It was either very late or very early when Izzy woke up and couldn't go back to sleep. Careful not to wake Lug, she stood up and tiptoed over the boulder until the sound of his snoring faded. She sat down on the giant's skull's smooth forehead. The sky was full of stars, like someone had tossed a handful of sugar out into the night.

The trilling of insects filled the darkness. Izzy took off her hat and set it in her lap. She shut her eyes. It was just like being back in Everton, sitting on the side porch in that wicker chair the night before Hen disappeared—the night she had wished for an adventure and to be as far away from home and family as possible. She looked out at the stars and tried to feel if that fragile thread between Hen and her still existed.

"Are you still there?" she whispered. "Please tell me you are!"

"Is who still there?"

Izzy spun around. A wolf stood behind her. For a half second, she forgot who it was and nearly screamed.

"You scared me," she said with an exhale.

Moonlight glinted off Selden's fangs as he grinned. "Sorry. Sometimes I forget which form I'm in." He shook his coat and Changed back into a boy. He walked over and sat down a few feet from Izzy. "You were thinking about your sister, huh?"

She nodded.

"I guess she's lucky."

"What do you mean?"

Selden picked at the loose threads of his trouser cuffs. "You know, that she's got someone who cares about her so much. Before I went to Earth, I thought that's what all families did."

Izzy waited for him to say something sarcastic or mean. After all, the last time they spoke, they'd screamed at each other. But he just sat there, winding the strings around his fingers. It seemed like a heavy cloud had gathered over his usually bright eyes.

"Selden, what was your human family like?" Izzy asked.

He shrugged. "Didn't get much of a chance to find out." He paused, then added, "They didn't want me."

"Oh," said Izzy. "I thought you ran away."

"I did, but only after I heard them say they were going to send me to a—what's that word? Orpher...orphor—"

"Orphanage." Based on what Lug had just told her, Izzy realized this meant Selden had been orphaned twice. She ran her fingers around the brim of her hat. Why was it so much easier to talk in the dark? She found words coming to her lips that she couldn't even bear to think about in the daytime. "You're wrong, you know. My sister's not lucky to have me at all. The last time I talked to Hen, we got in a huge fight. I said terrible, terrible things to her. If that's the last memory she has of me, if I never get the chance to make it right..." She glanced at Selden, expecting one of his smug grins.

Instead, his face was serious. "If you don't make it right, you'll regret it every day for the rest of your life."

He leaned back and tilted his face to the stars that were quickly disappearing into the lightening sky. When he spoke again, the swagger was back in his voice. "Look, it's no secret we'd both love to be rid of each other, right?"

Izzy raised an eyebrow but didn't answer.

"I guess we're going to have to wait a little longer to get our wish," said Selden. "The three of us are coming to Avhalon now."

Izzy sat up straighter. "Are you serious? What made you change your mind?"

Selden looked behind him at his sleeping friends and lowered his voice. "When your sister disappeared, you said there was no Changeling to take her place, right?"

"Right..."

"That's because aside from the three of us, there aren't any more Changelings left in Faerie to do the job."

Izzy let his words sink in for a moment. "What happened to them? Was it the Unglers?"

"Yes, sort of. The Unglers hunt Changelings, but they're working for someone else. They're working for Morvanna."

"Morvanna? Who is that?"

"She's the new queen in Avhalon." Selden sneered. "At least that's what she makes everyone call her."

"This is the woman you and Shank were talking about, right?" *The same woman I heard you and Dree whispering about back at Yawning Top*, she thought.

Selden nodded. "A few years ago, she showed up in Avhalon, took over everything, and built a huge castle for herself. Then she brought in the Unglers from who knows where and sent them out to round up all the Changelings they could find. No one knows what she did with them. They just disappeared."

"Why didn't the three of you disappear too?"

Selden shifted. A painful look flashed across his face. "I didn't return from Earth until after it all happened," he said. "When I heard about the Unglers, I hid myself in the Edgewood. When Lug and Dree came back to Faerie, I found them before anyone else did, and we've been hiding out together ever since."

Selden stood up. The cloud still lingered over his face, but his eyes shone fiercely. "We'd almost given up on ever finding the others. But if the Piper took your sister, then maybe there's one Changeling still alive to take her place. Maybe they're *all* still alive. The Apple Festival is our best chance to find out what really happened to them. There'll be all sorts of fairies there, and it'll be easy for us to blend in with the crowd."

Izzy remembered what Dree said back at Yawning Top, how she thought the Piper was working for Morvanna. "This means Hen is with Morvanna too. Do you think she's OK?"

"I don't know," said Selden. "Morvanna's become very powerful. They say there's not a fairy that can match her this side of the mountains."

Selden must have seen the worry on Izzy's face, because he quickly added, "Your sister is probably just fine. Morvanna wants Changelings, not humans. You'll find out more when you get to the city."

"What does Dree think of your plan?"

"Hates it, of course. But we haven't got many options now that the Unglers found Yawning Top. I promised her that if we don't find anything out about the other Changelings, we'll leave Avhalon straight away." He sighed and lowered his head. "Faerie's big enough that you can spend your whole life looking for new places to hide out."

The stars were gone, replaced by the pale lemon sky of morning. Selden walked out to the far edge of the giant's skull. "Hey, come here. I'll show you where we're going."

Izzy got to her feet and joined him. They faced west, away from the rising sun. From their position, Izzy could see that the Edgewood stood on top of a huge plateau. The Giant's Boneyard lay at the plateau's rim, at the very border of the forest. To either side of them, the line of trees ran on like a curling green ribbon. Below them, a grassy plain rolled out for miles to the feet of a chain of lavender mountains.

Cradled at the base of the tallest peak, Izzy saw a city that she knew must be Avhalon. The morning sunlight danced off the towers of an enormous castle in the center of the city. It sat atop an outcropping of stone at the junction of two rivers that rushed down from the mountains.

Selden pointed at the mountain range. "Those are the Avhals. Mount Mooring is the tallest one you can see from here. And the two rivers that flow around it are the Noy and the Liadan. See where they join together? That big river runs all the way south to the Gray Sea."

The city's stone walls rose high above the water, surrounded on almost all sides by the rivers.

Izzy remembered the story of King Arthur's final resting place and smiled to herself. "Avhalon. The Isle of Apples," she said.

Selden tilted his head to one side. "I guess it does look like an island from up here, doesn't it?"

"I'm almost there, Hen," Izzy whispered. "Just hold on a little longer."

Selden cleared his throat. "You know, since we've got to travel on together a little longer, maybe we should call a truce."

He held out his hand. Even in his boy form, he had a wolfish smile. "If I promise not to play any more tricks?"

Izzy considered saying something sarcastic, but she was too happy to be annoyed with him anymore. Knowing that she wouldn't have to go to Avhalon alone made her feel light enough to float right into the air. She plopped the hat back on and took his hand.

"OK. Truce."

THE APPLE FESTIVAL

BY LATE AFTERNOON OF the next day, Izzy sat with her legs hanging out the back of a dwarf's wagon. On one side of her sat a skinny man with curly black hair who kept calling her his "sweet little daughter," because he knew it annoyed her. On the other side of her sat a very large woman with a scarf tied around her face to hide her large tufts of neck hair. A delicate white butterfly rested on Izzy's shoulder, almost invisible in the bright afternoon sun.

"Oof, this shirt is too tight!" said the woman, stuffing her ample bosom back inside her tunic. "Oh, why did I have to be the mother?"

"Lug, will you stop complaining?" hissed the man on the other side of Izzy. "A family looks much less suspicious than four kids traveling alone. And stop messing with your bust, or I'll start laughing, and then I'll never be able to hold on to this Likeness!"

"Both of you hush!" said the butterfly. "We're about to cross the Liadan Bridge!"

The wagon's wheels clattered against smooth, gray stones as they started up onto the bridge. Izzy could hear the sounds of water rushing beneath them.

"It'll be faster to go the rest of the way on foot," said Selden, hopping down off the back of the wagon. "Come on, family of mine! Thank you kindly for the ride," he called to the dwarf, whose pony looked very relieved when it saw Lug get off.

Lug helped Izzy hop down, and they joined the throng of fairies funneling over the bridge to enter the city gates. It took Izzy every effort not to stare. They were surrounded by every kind of fairy she'd ever read about, and plenty that she'd never even imagined: all sorts of elves, pixies, dwarves, a dozen giants twice as tall as Lug, brownies that looked like they could be Shank's cousins, and winged sprites zipping between them all. There were also a few races of talking animals: mice, a black bear wearing an eye patch, and three incredibly old-looking goats. If Izzy wasn't so worried about finding Hen, it would have been the most amazing day of her life.

Beside them, a man carted a huge hive in a wheelbarrow with a swarm of tiny, winged fairies buzzing all around it. A sign on the hive said, *Pollening Honey—For Sale by the Jar.*

Izzy tried not to gape as she pointed out the hive to the butterfly on her shoulder. "What's pollening honey taste like?"

Dree shrugged as if nothing could be more ordinary than

honey made by a hundred Tinker Bells. "It's all right. Goes good with pancakes."

All sorts of smells from the sweaty crowd hovered in the humid air: musky barnyard odors mixed with pine and incense. Izzy touched the necklace of Scarlet Stairstep hidden under her shirt.

She reached up for Lug's hand. "Will there be any you-know-what here?" she whispered, thinking of the Unglers.

"I wouldn't think they'd show their snouts here," he whispered back. "They'd scare everyone to death. It'd cause a stampede." As they approached the stone entryway into the city, he wiped a tear from the corner of his eye. "Coming home at last! Thought I'd never see this place again."

Dree flew to his cheek and flicked him with her wing. "Shhh! This isn't home, not anymore. And we've all got to be careful. Take a look at that!"

Izzy's eyes followed her as she fluttered up toward the archway at the end of the bridge. Two tall guards in dark-green uniforms stood on either side of the arch. They were as tall as full-grown men, with sallow, pockmarked skin and sharp teeth protruding up from their lips. Each carried a short sword and a club in his belt, and they patted them threateningly as they stared down their long, twisty noses at the crowd.

"Goblins," whispered Lug.

Selden eyed the guards, then elbowed a fairy man walking beside him. "Say, friend. I h'ain't been to a festival in a couple years," he drawled. "What's with them tall fellas?" He pointed his chin at the guards.

The man answered with his hand over his mouth, speaking so low that Izzy could barely hear. "Wevildale goblins," he said. "*She* brought 'em in from the Norlorn Mountains. Says they're here to keep order, but don't look at 'em wrong, or they'll reorder your face."

Izzy pulled her hat down tighter and squeezed Lug's hand. She let out a breath of relief when they finally passed under the archway.

The flow of the crowd carried them forward through the narrow city streets. On either side, brightly painted wooden buildings tilted this way and that, like they had been built on top of each other over the years without much thought to style or stability. Some houses had round windows, some square, and some had tiny doors no larger than a deck of cards. Izzy thought they looked cheerful in a ramshackle sort of way.

The castle gave her an entirely different feeling. It loomed oppressively over everything, like it was looking down, watching her as she passed. From her view back in the Edgewood, Avhalon had looked like a city that belonged nestled in the clouds. But the longer she looked at it, the more Izzy thought the castle seemed out of place, too new and perfect compared with the other buildings. Its towers soared hundreds of feet above the rest of the town, casting everything beneath it into dark shadows. Their pointed rooftops looked like silver claws grabbing for the sun. Was Hen at the top of one of those towers? Izzy didn't see a single crack or crevice that could serve as a toehold in the sheer walls, and the lowest window was at least a hundred feet off the ground.

The sun had begun to set as the crowd wound its way behind the castle and onto a wide, grassy field that lay between Avhalon and the base of Mount Mooring. Rows of twisty apple trees ringed the field on all sides. A full moon floated overhead, lost among the lanterns hanging from their black branches.

The many vendors Izzy had seen on their journey had set up booths on the field in the center of the orchard. They sold trinkets and art, livestock and tools, and lots and lots of food.

Lug breathed in deep. "Ah, the sweet smells of paradise!"

"Lug's version of paradise is a never-ending, deep-fat fryer," said Selden.

Izzy laughed. For a moment, she forgot why she was there and let herself get swept up in the festival atmosphere.

Jugglers and fire-breathers and barefoot dancers whirled around her. She stared in wonder at the array of clothes for sale—bridal veils embroidered with morning dew, a hunting cloak the color of shadows, leather gloves that let you stick your hands straight into a fire and not get burned. There were booths hawking potions in glass bottles: *Love Detangler, Colic Cure, Grump Reducer, Weed Shriveler*. Magic infused everything Izzy saw. But it was a humble sort of magic, country magic practiced by country fairies.

Lug wandered out among the food stalls, pretending to inspect what was on sale. When he joined Izzy and Selden again, he pulled a handful of crumbly apple pastries out of his blouse. Izzy took one and shoved it into her mouth. It was flaky, sweet, tart, and buttery all at once. She didn't know if it had been baked by magic, and she didn't care. It was the most heavenly thing she'd ever eaten.

Dree landed on Izzy's shoulder and stamped her butterfly feet. "Lug, you've got to quit doing that! You're going to get caught!"

"But being a woman makes me so hungry!" he mumbled through a mouth full of apple dumpling. "Besides, everyone's enjoying themselves too much to notice."

"They won't enjoy it for long," Dree grumbled. "This thick air means it's going to rain on all their heads before the night's over. Lug! You get back over here right now!"

He ignored her and went back to the pastry stands. Dree lifted off from Izzy's shoulder and flitted after him.

Izzy licked the last crumbs off her fingers and walked out into the crowd. Straight ahead, a tall figure wearing a crumpled hat bobbed among the other fairies. A crop of short white hair peeked out from beneath the cap.

Izzy stared in shock. It couldn't be.

"Marian?" she whispered.

Izzy turned away from Selden and pushed into the crowd. She followed after the cap, weaving between the fairies, trying to keep up. It looked exactly like Marian's hat. But how could she have gotten away from the cobwebs? The crowd thickened, and Izzy lost sight of her.

Izzy wiped the sweat off her forehead. She must have been imagining things. Marian couldn't have escaped Netherbee Hall, not after what Izzy had seen. She patted the tiny bottle in her jacket pocket. Her mind had played a trick on her, letting her see what she wanted to see.

Izzy turned this way and that as the crowd swirled around her. Perfect. Now she'd lost Selden and the others too. She was just about to turn and go looking for them when she heard something that made her skin go prickly all over: a flute playing a tune, sad and sweet. She knew it instantly.

It was the same song playing in the woods when Hen disappeared.

A throng of fairies had gathered in the center of the grassy field. Izzy pushed her way through them to get closer to the music. The crowd parted to let a black horse step past. On his back rode a slender man, pale as a swan. Compared to the common fairies at the festival, he was dressed like a prince. He even wore a thin crown of silver set into his dark hair.

Izzy's stomach did backflips. "Good Peter," she whispered to herself.

The Piper continued past, riding toward a line of tall white tents at the far end of the field. If he was here, that meant her sister must be here too. Izzy had to tell the Changelings. They'd help her find Hen.

Trumpets blasted from the direction of the castle. Everyone turned to look. Whispers rippled through the crowd as the fairies pressed back farther to make more room.

"It's her. It's her..."

"Here she comes! The queen!"

Four snow-white mares pulled an open carriage into the throng of gawking fairies. Wevildale goblins flanked the carriage on all sides, shoving away spectators who tried to get too close. Izzy's pulse thumped along in time to the trumpets as the queen drew nearer.

The woman standing in the carriage held herself as tall and stiff as the white towers of her castle. Her red hair was parted down the middle and fell stick-straight to the middle of her back. She could have been a statue if not for that hair, swishing to the rhythm of the carriage, and eyes that darted around the crowd like a reptile's. They rested for a brief moment on each fairy before moving to the next face.

The carriage rolled to a stop a dozen yards from where Izzy stood. The crowd seemed to press forward and draw back at the same time. Izzy felt it too. She wanted to keep a safe distance, but she couldn't take her eyes off the queen. Izzy had the weird feeling she had seen her somewhere before.

Morvanna held out both hands to quiet the crowd. She waited, letting the silence build before she spoke. "Good evening, my dear citizens of Avhalon." She clipped her words like a gardener cutting thorn bushes. "And greetings to our guests from near and far. As your queen, I welcome you to the Festival of the Apples. As you know, it is tradition to open the festival with the Adoption Ceremony."

The fairies standing around Izzy nodded and murmured in agreement.

"As it happens, this year, we have only one human child to choose from..."

Izzy leaned forward onto her toes.

"...and so I have decided to start a new tradition." Morvanna smiled coyly. "This year, I have decided to adopt the child for my own!"

The queen stepped aside with a dramatic swoosh of her emerald skirts. Someone sat in the carriage beside her. Izzy jammed the back of her hand into her mouth to keep from crying out.

It was Hen.

QUIET AS A MOUSE

IZZY GAPED AT THE girl standing next to Morvanna. This was not her milk-mustachioed sister with grass stains on her knees. This was Hen, the princess.

She wore a plum-colored silk dress. Her usually tangled curls had been tamed into perfect ringlets. She waved excitedly to the applauding crowd, blowing them kisses. Izzy couldn't believe it. She was close enough that Hen would be able to hear her if she called out, but she knew she couldn't do it. Goblins surrounded the carriage on all sides. She just had to sit there and watch as Morvanna reached down and petted Hen's hair as sweetly as their own mother.

Morvanna raised one muscled arm, and the crowd snapped silent. "Back to your revelry, my good fairies. Let this mark the official beginning of our jubilations!"

Morvanna nodded down at Hen, who reached into a little basket and flung a handful of flower petals out at the crowd.

Morvanna put her open hand beneath her lips and blew gently. The petals spun in midair, then morphed into a cluster of golden coins that jingled against each other as they fell and landed on the grass. A greedy roar went up through the crowd as fairies rushed forward to grab up the coins. Morvanna barked an order to her driver, and the carriage continued on, drawing all the fairies along behind it.

Izzy tried to follow them. "No!" The words came out before she could stop them. "Please, wait!"

The fairies around Izzy stepped away from her and stared down at her suspiciously. They began whispering.

"What's she squawkin' 'bout?"

"Someone oughta find her ma and pa…"

The goblins in the rear of Morvanna's entourage turned and craned their necks, looking curiously at the small crowd gathered around Izzy.

Izzy pulled her hat down tight and tried to back away, but the crowd stood thick around her on all sides. She saw one of the goblin guards moving toward her. She turned and shoved her way through the throng. She searched for the Changelings, but she didn't dare call out their names. Oh, why hadn't she stayed close to them? She was hopelessly turned around now.

In the time since Morvanna had made her appearance, the center of the field had turned into a giant dance party. A sea of fairies twirled in time to the music of a fiddle band. Izzy glanced over her shoulder. She spotted the dark green of a goblin uniform.

Izzy plunged into the middle of the field of dancing fairies. She dashed through the whirling bodies, pushing past them toward the apple orchard. The booths at this end of the festival had emptied out. Everyone must have joined in the dancing. A cider stand had a wooden sign hanging from the front that read, *Back Soone. No Free Refills*. Izzy circled behind the stall and ducked behind a row of wooden barrels. She looked back at the way she came. No goblin. She had lost him.

Even away from the crowd, the air was thick and hot. She slumped against a large burlap sack stamped with the word, *Chestnuts*. She needed to figure out what to do next, but she was too flustered to think clearly.

Over the sound of the fiddle music, Izzy heard harsh voices drawing close. She peeked around the other side of the barrels. Three goblin guards stalked toward her. Two were tall and gangly; the third was a greasy, short goblin with a nose covered in shiny pimples. Izzy's pulse raced. Should she run away? But where to? She knew they hadn't seen her yet, so she opened up the sack of chestnuts and wriggled inside. She cinched the top shut with the drawstring.

Still as a mouse, still as a tiny mouse, she told herself. She held her breath as still as she could, imagining she was no larger than a handful of chestnuts.

"Looks like there ain't no one here," said one of the guards.

"Guess that means this cider's free for the taking!" said another, chuckling.

"Shut yer traps, the both of you," said the third. "Hmm… we shoulda brought more hands. You two grab a barrel each. I'll carry us back some vittles."

Izzy's stomach dropped as the sack she was in lifted onto what she assumed was the shoulder of the short guard. The chestnuts clattered all around her. She took shallow, mousy breaths and tried not to move.

"Oof, this is heavy!" complained the short goblin. "Come on, you lazy grunts! We're supposed to be on duty. Grab yer barrels, and let's be off before we're missed."

The goblins hoisted up their loads and shuffled off into the night. Izzy couldn't guess where they were headed. She had a horrible vision of the sack being opened and of staring into the angry faces of a dozen hungry goblins. Did goblins eat children? From the look of their jagged teeth, it seemed possible.

The sack was made from rough cloth, worn thin in certain spots. She could tell by the absence of light that they must have headed away from the brightly lit field and were probably circling behind the booths and stalls. The goblins grumbled and cursed as they bumped into each other in the dark.

"Shhh!" hissed the short guard who carried Izzy. "Be quiet, you rodents. We're about to walk past Her Majesty's tent."

The guards slowed to a tiptoe. With a crash, one of them

tripped on something and fell into his companion. Izzy heard them tumble onto the ground and curse as they dropped their barrels.

From somewhere close by, a woman's voice said, "What was that? Peter, go and have a look."

"You've done it now, idiot!" whispered one of the guards. "You know what she did to Gristle? She conjured up them ants, and they ate him alive!"

"Me? It was yer fault. Don't matter though—we're done for!"

There was a swishing of canvas, then a flood of yellow light.

"Ah, Blister," said a man's genteel voice. "Her Majesty and I were just talking about you. Won't you come in and join us?"

The short goblin gulped and mumbled a "Yes, sir."

He stepped forward and dropped the sack. Izzy stifled a grunt as she fell hard onto the ground. Boots clomped away from her, and the yellow light disappeared.

As she lay there in the darkness, Izzy realized she had just been plopped right outside Morvanna's tent.

THE FAIRY QUEEN

IZZY WORKED HER FINGERS into the neck of the sack until she got it loose. She brushed the dusty chestnuts away from her face and gulped fresh air. The fiddlers were still playing up a frenzy, but they sounded farther away now. Blister must have dropped her on the back side of the queen's tent. Izzy opened the sack wider and peeked out. She faced rows of gnarled, black apple trees. A large tent stood on the other side of her, only a few yards away. Blurry shadows swam across the canvas. If that was Morvanna's tent, then Hen must be in there too.

Izzy took a deep breath and gripped the sack tight in both hands. Careful not to rattle the chestnuts, she rolled slowly toward the tent until the canvas brushed her nose. She pressed the side of her head into the grass. With one finger, she lifted the canvas just enough to see underneath.

The three goblins stood in a line with their backs to Izzy, shifting nervously on their feet. The man with the genteel voice was Good Peter. He sat with one leg sprawled lazily over the arm of a chair, looking very bored. Morvanna sat on a padded stool in front of a dressing table, combing her long, red tresses over and over. Next to the mirror, a black-and-yellow finch hopped about inside a wire cage.

Morvanna tore off a scrap of pastry from her half-eaten plate of food and held it out to the little bird. She swiveled to face the goblins. She stared at them icily, not saying anything.

It was too much for Blister, who dropped to one knee and bowed his head. "Our humblest, deepest, sincerest apologies, Your Majesty. We'll go right back to our posts. We'll patrol the crowd, just like you asked."

Morvanna glared at Blister, picking at the corner of her thumbnail with her forefinger. For a long moment, the tent was quiet except for the sound of her scratching.

"Come closer," she said finally. The goblin stumbled forward. "Blister, you've been sloppy, and you know how I feel about sloppiness. Perhaps I should find you an easier task. Maybe I could put you in charge of the ants. Just like your friend, Gristle…"

"Oh, n-no, Your Majesty," he stammered. "That…that won't be needed, your most majestic Majesty!"

Morvanna thumped him between the eyes. "Then get back to work!" She turned back to the mirror on her table and resumed grooming herself. "If I learn that you miss something, I'll send you right back to the Norlorns just in time for troll-hatching season."

The three goblins blurted out a simultaneous "Yes, Your Majesty." They scurried out through the flap at the front of the tent.

Morvanna pulled her hair back into a tight coil. She took a gold hairpin from her table and jabbed it into the bun to hold it in place. "There, that's lovely, don't you think so, Peter?"

The candlelight flickered in Peter's large black eyes. From this close, they reminded Izzy more of a wild animal's eyes than a man's. "Your Majesty is the pinnacle of regal beauty," he said.

Not really, thought Izzy. She'd seen hundreds of illustrations of storybook queens with "regal beauty," and Morvanna didn't fit the description at all. Her strong build seemed better fit for chopping wood than sitting on a throne. Queens were supposed to be elegant, confident. But Morvanna's eyes flitted nervously around the room. Her fingers never stopped moving, fixing and straightening things on her table. Worse, she kept pick, pick, picking at the same spot on her thumb.

"Blister, that imbecile," growled Morvanna. "I should come up with some elaborate torture for him just to remind the rest of them to stay on their toes."

"You proved your point with Gristle," said Peter, shining his flute on the lapel of his jacket. "Don't waste your powers on those goblins. You should conserve your precious resources."

Morvanna pinched her lips together. "Mmm, I suppose you're right. Besides, my pets will leave their hiding places at midnight to search the festival themselves. Those lazy goblins might miss something, but I can assure you that my Unglers won't."

Izzy's breath caught in her throat. The Unglers were coming to the festival? But why? She had to warn the Changelings. She didn't know what time it was, but midnight couldn't be far off.

Peter looked disinterested. "Mmm, yes, I'm sure they will be most thorough."

"Oh, they will. Once they pick up a trail, they don't stop until they've caught their prey."

Peter arched one eyebrow. "Are you keeping a secret from me?"

"The Ungler troop I sent into the Edgewood returned this morning," said Morvanna, smiling. "They found Changelings!"

"What?" Peter's flute clattered to the ground. He stood and swooped it up again. "But that's not possible. You've had the Edgewood watched for years. We both agreed it was useless to keep looking there."

"You always want to give up too easily," said Morvanna, turning back to her mirror. She fed the finch another piece of bread. "I knew if we kept looking, we would find them. There were three, possibly four of them. The little brats only barely got away. The Unglers said they were headed west. Where else would they be going but to Avhalon? I told you bringing back this stupid festival was a good idea. Fairies can't resist this sort of thing. I bet those Changelings are out there, mingling in the crowd as we speak!"

Every muscle in Izzy's body tensed. The whole Apple Festival was one big trap her friends had walked right into. She cupped one hand behind her ear, straining to hear more of Morvanna's plan.

Peter tapped his thigh with his flute. "Don't be so sure about all this. Your Unglers don't always get it right. After all, they led me up to that house on Earth, but when I got there, all I found was Henrietta."

"My Unglers don't make mistakes," snapped Morvanna. "If they smelled Changeling, then there's one there. And as soon as this is all over, you're going right back up to search again." She scratched at her thumbnail again. The horrid, digging motion made her whole arm twitch. "There's something else. The Unglers found the Changelings' hideout in the Edgewood. It's a tree covered in Scarlet Stairstep."

Peter wrinkled his nose as if he'd just taken a whiff of the red mushrooms. Izzy touched the strand around her neck nervously.

"Clever little urchins," snarled Morvanna. "But now that we know their trick, they won't be able to hide for long."

So the Unglers and Peter were working together, and not just in the Edgewood. They were hunting for Changelings on Earth too. When Peter found Hen, he must have assumed she was the Changeling the Unglers smelled. They must have picked up on Marian's scent by mistake.

Morvanna glanced at Peter and let out an annoyed huff. "Stop looking so depressed. It's not like you won't get paid for your work." Her eyes flicked to his expensive suit. "Another trip to Earth will hardly be wasted. If for whatever reason you can't find a Changeling, you can always bring me another human child. The girl may not be what I was looking for, but she does have her uses."

Peter folded his arms. "I can't just snatch up humans like they were stray cats. The rules of the Exchange clearly state there must be a one-to-one trade."

"As if you cared for rules," said Morvanna, rolling her eyes. "What about Hamelin?"

"Don't believe that old story. I traded those townspeople for their children fair and square. It's not my fault they didn't want what they got. I learned my lesson though. It's best if humans don't know when they're getting the switch. But a switch is *always* made."

Morvanna slammed her fist on her table. The finch chirped and fluttered against the bars of its cage. "You're always telling me no!" Izzy held still as a stone as she watched Morvanna rise from her stool and approach Peter. The skin around her thumbnail had split open, but she didn't stop picking at it. "You always have some excuse, some reason why I can't do what I want! When I want to use my power, you tell me to save it. When I want more Changelings, you tell me they're all gone. And now you tell me you can't even bring me one more measly human?" Morvanna now stood face-to-face with Peter. He was a tall man, but she appeared to tower over him. "Maybe that crown is going to your head. Maybe you're confused as to who is ruler and who is servant."

Peter tapped his neck like he was checking it was still there. "Your Majesty is overexcited," he said with a flattering smile. "You know I only want what's best for you. If you want more humans, then of course, you shall have them."

Morvanna stepped back from him and wiped her bleeding thumb on her skirt. She exhaled as she sat back down. "You've been very useful to me, Peter. I couldn't have done any of this without you. I've rewarded you handsomely, haven't I?"

Peter touched his crown with one finger and bowed.

"Good. Now, I want to see the girl. Bring her out."

Peter opened his mouth to say something but thought better of it. He nodded and ducked under a flap that led to an adjacent tent. Finally—Izzy was about to see her sister. She lifted the tent canvas ever so slightly so she could see a little better.

A moment later, Peter came back, leading a sleepy-looking Hen by the hand. Her hair was a nest of tangles, and she'd buttoned her nightgown wrong. Hen hung back when she saw Morvanna, but Peter whispered something softly to her that made her walk forward.

Izzy ground her teeth as she watched the queen hold out her arms to her sister.

"There, there, my little princess," cooed Morvanna as she

folded Hen into an embrace. "That bad old Peter woke you, didn't he? But cheer up. Here's something I know you'll like."

The queen reached for a candle on the vanity and held it up in front of Hen. Hen's eyes widened excitedly as she watched the wavering flame.

"Yes, that's pretty, isn't it?" said Morvanna, placing the candle on the ground at Hen's feet. "But I'm sure Peter can make it even lovelier."

Peter reached into his coat pocket and pulled out his silver flute. He began to play a simple, happy tune. The flame stretched and grew until it looked like a fiery little man with a spike of flickering hair. He gave Hen a gentlemanly bow. She smiled.

Peter picked up the pace of his tune, and the fire man crossed his arms and kicked up his heels in a dance. Peter ran the notes down the scale, and the little man tumbled off the candle wick onto his bottom. Hen giggled and clapped her hands.

"Yes, that's it," said Morvanna gently. "Our little princess likes your tricks, Peter." She reached behind her and picked up a black glass vial from a tray on the vanity.

Peter directed the fire man to do ever sillier tricks, stumbling head over feet and knocking his head against the ground. Hen laughed harder.

Slowly, Morvanna stood up behind her. She held the ebony vial in one hand. Izzy stiffened.

As Hen laughed, the queen waved her fingers like she was

wafting smoke upward into the vial. Izzy couldn't see any-thing in the air above Hen's head, but Morvanna was clearly gathering some invisible substance into the bottle. After a few moments, she plugged it with a stopper and replaced it on the vanity table. Hen still giggled as she watched the fire man. She didn't seem to be harmed. Izzy let out a tense breath.

"That's enough music," said Morvanna. "My little blossom needs her sleep." She poured her cup of wine onto the fire man. He sizzled and vanished.

"Hey!" said Hen.

Morvanna pressed two fingers over Hen's lips. "Now, now, no arguments. A kiss and then back to bed with you, my love." She bent down, and Hen gave her a quick peck on the cheek before letting Peter lead her back to her own tent.

The queen waited until they were gone. She turned back to her dressing table and wiped her cheek with the back of her hand. Izzy lifted her head another inch off the ground to see what Morvanna was doing. The queen bent over a stone bowl on the table. She held the vial up to the light, then tilted it into the bowl. She opened a small velvet bag on her dressing table and withdrew a strand of burgundy thread. The contents in the bowl hissed as she dropped the thread into it. A thin wisp of vapor rose up. Izzy heard what sounded like the muted scream of a child.

Morvanna raised the bowl to her lips and drained it. She set it down and clutched at her throat, gagging and coughing.

When the fit passed, she leaned toward the mirror and patted the corners of her eyes with her middle fingers. Peter returned. The queen spun to face him. Izzy held back a gasp of surprise.

Morvanna looked years younger. Even the fine lines at the corners of her eyes were gone. She still was no beauty, but she radiated youth and energy. Again, something familiar about Morvanna's face drew Izzy in and kept her from looking away.

Even Peter seemed impressed. "Very nice. The girl laughs so easily. Why not just use her to make as much elixir as you want?"

Morvanna sighed like a teacher impatient with a slow pupil. "Human laughter lends the potion a certain charm." She gestured to her rosy cheeks. "But the elixir's true strength can only come from Changeling heart." The queen reached up and opened the birdcage. The finch trembled in her hand as she drew him out. "Only a few more Changelings and I'll have enough hearts to make a concentrated batch. Then there'll be no more need to 'conserve resources,' will there?"

Izzy felt frozen in place. She wanted to get up and run to her friends, to warn them of the danger they were in. But her sister was almost within reach. She couldn't leave without Hen, not now that she was so close.

Morvanna cupped the finch gently against her chest as she sprinkled a dusting of salt on the surface of her table. When she spoke again, it was in a dreamy, faraway voice. "All those years of hard work…so much time I thought I wasted… It was all leading up to this moment."

Morvanna set the shivering bird on the pile of salt. She kept one finger firmly on its back so it couldn't fly away. She breathed on the salt like a girl fogging a glass on a cold day. The salt swirled. It formed a white, ghostly substance, more solid than smoke, but just as fluid.

Cobwebs.

The frightened bird beat its wings, but before it could rise from the table, a wisp of cobweb coiled around its feet. More tendrils reached up like tentacles and lashed around the finch. Izzy couldn't watch. She shut her eyes. The fluttering sounds slowed, then stopped altogether. When Izzy opened her eyes again, Morvanna was leaning into the mirror, putting on lipstick.

"Now, I suppose we should go out and make an appearance at our own party," she said to Peter. "You'll come, won't you? I hate this sort of thing, and I need someone to make me laugh."

"That is my specialty, Your Majesty." Peter offered the queen his arm, and they exited together.

On the dressing table lay a tightly wrapped ball of white, silent and still as a cocoon.

THE CHICKEN THIEF
STEALS A HEN

Izzy COUNTED TO FIVE slowly before squirming out of the sack. She lifted the tent canvas with both hands and rolled underneath. Inside, the candle on Morvanna's dressing table flickered as she walked past. She crept to the opening where she'd seen Peter take Hen. She listened for a few moments but didn't hear anything on the other side of the curtain. She drew it back and went inside.

It took a moment for her eyes to adjust to the darkness. The festival lanterns projected the shadow of a goblin guard onto the tent's canvas. Izzy jumped, then realized he was outside of the tent, pacing back and forth. Hen lay in the center of the room on a lush pile of mattresses. Izzy tiptoed to the edge of the bed and watched her sister sleeping. Her stomach twisted at the thought of Morvanna standing behind Hen, harvesting her laughter. What if she'd done some sort of permanent damage? But Hen looked exactly the same as before.

Actually, now she looked like a little princess, straight out of a storybook. What if she didn't want to come home at all?

Ever since Izzy had left Yawning Top, she had been rehearsing what to say when she saw her sister, if she ever saw her again. Now that Hen was only a few inches away, all her rehearsals went out the window. There were only two words that mattered, and as long as she could get them out, she could deal with whatever might come next.

She took a deep breath and gently tapped Hen's cheek.

Hen stirred, then blinked her eyes open. She sat up and looked at Izzy, confused. "Are Mom and Dad here?" she mumbled.

"No, it's just me."

Those words must not have been very comforting, because tears welled up in Hen's eyes. "I—I want to go home," she whimpered.

Relief washed over Izzy. She reached out her arms, and Hen's sleepy head fell onto her shoulder.

"I'm sorry, I'm sorry, I'm sorry…" While Hen cried softly, Izzy said the two words over and over until they sounded like nonsense. Her little sister felt so much smaller than she remembered. She rubbed Hen's back and tried to imagine what their mom would say if she were there. "Shhh, don't cry, clucky Hen."

Hen sniffled and looked up at her. "You smell like Dad's gym bag."

Izzy laughed and hugged her closer. "I'm going to take you

home, I promise." She pulled away from Hen's embrace and looked in her eyes. "But first we need to get out of here. We've got to work together, OK?"

Hen wiped the snot off her face with her nightgown sleeve. "Is this like a mission?"

"Yes, that's exactly what it is," said Izzy. She knew Hen loved missions. "Our mission is to get out of here before Morvanna comes back. You know this place better than me. Which way do we go?"

Before Hen could answer, the goblin's silhouette on the tent grew larger and larger. The shadow bent down to lift up the corner of the tent flap.

"Hurry, get down!" whispered Hen.

Izzy dropped behind Hen's mattresses and flattened herself onto the ground.

The goblin ducked into the dark tent. "Thought I heard voices."

"That was me," said Hen, sliding off her bed onto the floor. "I was talking to myself, saying how I'm so hungry I could eat my own arm."

"Hungry?" growled the goblin. "You just had your supper. And lots of it too."

Izzy inched forward until she could just barely see around the corner of the mattress. Hen stood with her feet planted apart and her arms crossed, staring up at a goblin guard more than twice her size.

"Well, I'm hungry again," Hen whined. "I want a fried apple tart!"

The goblin sneered down his long nose at Hen. "I don't care what you want. What you *need* is to get back to bed." He bared pointed, yellow teeth and clacked them at her menacingly.

Hen didn't budge. She wrinkled her nose and leaned forward. "If you don't get me a fried apple tart right this minute, I'll tell Morvanna you're making me sad. And you *know* how she feels about me getting sad."

The guard's nostrils flared. "Fine," he spat. "Wouldn't want the little princess to be uncomfortable." He turned around and stomped out of the tent.

As soon as he was gone, Hen tiptoed back to Izzy's hiding spot.

Izzy hugged her sister. "I never thought I'd say this, but thank goodness for your whining!"

They hurried to the back of the tent, where they knelt, straining their ears for the sounds of guards on the other side. It felt like an eternity to Izzy, who was sure they'd be caught any second.

"Let's go, Hen. We can't wait any longer!"

The sisters wriggled out underneath the tent canvas. They stood up, facing the apple orchard. A sharp breeze blew out of the trees, slicing through the warm night. The leaves swished like a frightened whisper: *Go! Hurry!*

Izzy grabbed Hen's hand and ran. The fiddle music and merry sounds of the festival faded behind them as they sprinted through the rows of trees. Soon, they left the orchard behind and entered a forest of evergreens. The soft grass beneath their feet became steep, rocky ground. The sweet apple smell gave way to the sharp scent of pine. They were heading away from Avhalon, up the slopes of Mount Mooring.

The moon was full and high, giving them just enough light to weave through the tree trunks. Izzy's body dragged, and not just from running uphill. She'd done it. She'd found her sister and rescued her. She should have been thrilled. Instead, she felt a rising sense of dread.

Izzy stopped, nearly yanking Hen downhill.

"Hey…come on!" Hen said, panting and trying to pull Izzy along. "We can't…slow down now!"

They had stopped in front of a large, fallen fir tree. Izzy placed one hand on its trunk, trying to catch her breath. "Give me…just a minute… I need to think."

"No, no, we don't have time for that! Listen, Morvanna has these—these creatures, and she can train them to track anything she wants. If she tells them to come after me—"

"I know. I know what they can do."

Izzy felt pulled up the mountain and down it at the same time. Her sister needed her, but so did the Changelings. The Unglers would be out looking for them any minute, and the Scarlet Stairstep wouldn't protect them anymore. If she didn't warn them, they were as good as caught.

Izzy put both her hands on Hen's shoulders. "Hen, there's something I have to do. My friends need my help."

Hen looked shocked. "You have *friends*?"

"Yes, I do, and they're in trouble. I have to warn them. I have to tell them that Morvanna's planning—"

"I'm planning *what*?"

The voice sent a ragged chill down Izzy's spine. She spun around. A match scraped against stone, and a torch sputtered to life. Morvanna and Peter walked toward them with three goblins.

They'd been caught.

CAUGHT IN THE DARK

BLISTER HELD THE TORCH. Two other goblins—one thin, one stout—followed behind.

"There, Your Majesty!" said Blister, pointing straight at Izzy. "Just like I told you! I seen that girl take your little princess outta her tent."

Morvanna pushed Blister out of the way and walked closer to the girls. She looked down at Izzy, and her face relaxed. "Well, you were right, Blister. It's nothing but a little imp." The queen curled her finger at Izzy. "Come closer and let me get a better look at you."

Izzy gulped and took a step forward.

Morvanna's eyelids twitched as she picked at her thumb. "So, you little ragamuffin, what is all this about? What are you doing with my human?"

Hen leaned around Izzy. "She's not a ragamuffle. She's my sister!"

Morvanna grabbed Izzy by the shoulders, pulled off her hat, and tossed it away. When she saw Izzy's ears, she smiled greedily. "Look, Peter, it's true—another human child. You haven't been hiding this one from me, have you?"

Peter raised his eyebrows and tilted his head at Izzy. "No, Your Majesty. I have no idea how this child got here…"

"She came here to take me back home," said Hen.

Morvanna took Izzy's chin and jerked it up to the light. Her nails dug into the skin as she twisted Izzy's face back and forth. "Peter, you should be glad. This will save you from having to find me another human. Though this one is so small and sullen. I doubt her laughter is worth one tenth of her sister's."

As Peter stared at Izzy, a sudden change spread over his face. All his coolness melted away, replaced with a look of panic. "Your Majesty, give me charge of this one," he said, hurriedly taking Izzy's hand. "I'll lead her back to the castle with her sister…"

Izzy pulled away from him. "No, you have to let Hen go! She was stolen without a Changeling to take her place. And that's against the rules!"

"Now you sound just like Peter," Morvanna said with a sneer. "I can do what I like. I'm a queen, and you're a little nobody with a sullen face." She leaned forward and pursed her lips. She worked out a thin line of spittle that hung past her chin. Pinching it between her fingers, she pulled it down. It changed into a glistening chain as thin as a strand of silk. But

Izzy knew it was stronger than steel. It was the same chain the Unglers had used to snare Lug.

Morvanna tossed the finished chain to Blister. "Tie up the sister and bring her with us. Come along, Henrietta. It's time to go back." She reached out for Hen.

Izzy stepped in front of her, blocking her way.

Morvanna's face twisted in anger. "Why, you impudent little brat!" She slapped Izzy full across the face with the back of her hand so hard that she knocked Izzy backward, off her feet.

Stunned, Izzy propped herself up on one elbow and covered her face, expecting more blows. Morvanna dropped to her knees beside her, her eyes on Izzy's neck. When Izzy fell, the strand of Scarlet Stairstep had popped out from under her shirt.

Morvanna lifted the necklace up with one finger. Her eyes narrowed to slits as she leaned down. "*What* are you?"

Hen pounded Morvanna's back with her fists. "Get off of her! Let her go!"

Peter grabbed Hen around the waist and pulled her away. A shriek rang out in the darkness. Another high squeal, and another, scraped up the mountain toward them.

Morvanna smiled. She leaned closer and twisted Izzy's Stairstep necklace around her finger until the cord snapped. "What good timing," she whispered. Her breath smelled like burned meat. "My little pets can tell me exactly what you are."

Blister chuckled and held his torch out to the thin guard

behind him. "Take this. I'll tie up the ragamuffin. Hey! You listenin'? I said take the torch!"

The goblin didn't look at Blister. He looked down at Izzy and flashed a wolfish grin.

A white butterfly flew from the stout guard's shoulder and landed near Izzy's ear. "Now, Izzy!" it whispered. "Let's go!"

Izzy planted her boot on the soft spot below Morvanna's rib cage and kicked as hard as she could. The queen flew backward onto the ground. She rolled onto her hands and knees, clutching her stomach as she gasped for air.

"Your Majesty!" cried Peter. He let go of Hen and hurried to help the queen.

As Peter bent over, the big goblin kicked him in the back, making him fall right on top of Morvanna. Blister stumbled back, gaping uselessly as Selden and Lug both dropped their goblin Likenesses.

Selden Changed into a stag and knelt at Izzy's feet. "Let's get out of here! Come on!"

Hen's jaw dropped open. "Did you see what he just did?"

Izzy bent down to help Hen climb onto Selden's back. "I'll explain later!"

"Quickly, quickly!" said Dree, fluttering overhead.

More shrieks pierced the night. The hunched silhouettes of a dozen Unglers appeared out of the trees. They lumbered closer, grunting excitedly, like pigs in a frenzy.

Morvanna pushed Peter off and stood up, shaking with

fury. Blister cowered and shielded himself with the torch as she stretched her arm out to him. The sparks from the torch flew through the air and collected in her hands. She rolled them between her palms like a ball of clay until she held a sphere of glowing red flame.

Dree flew to one end of the fallen fir tree. She Changed back to herself and leaned against it with her shoulder. "Lug, help me!"

Lug Changed into an ox. Head down, he rammed into the log. As Morvanna held the fireball overhead, the log shuddered and rocked free of the ground. It rolled downhill, straight at the queen.

Morvanna threw herself out of harm's way, back to the ground. As she fell, she flung her fireball at Selden, but it veered wide into a stand of smaller trees that burst into flame. The rolling log slammed into three of the Unglers, dragging them with it down the mountain. The others leapt out of the way like bony cats.

Selden twisted his head around, nearly stabbing Izzy with his antlers. "Hurry up! Get on!"

Izzy scrambled onto Selden's back behind her sister. She barely had time to hold on before he took off up the mountain. Dree turned into a fawn, and Lug became a ram. They raced up the slope on either side of Selden.

The remaining Unglers were close behind. Their knuckles thudded the ground as they galloped. The fastest beast launched himself forward and swiped at Selden. Izzy cried out as its fingertips grazed her back. She looked over her shoulder.

Morvanna struggled out of Peter's grip, back to her feet. "Do something, you fool! They're getting away!" She collected another ball of flame in her hands and aimed it straight at the Changelings.

Izzy leaned forward, pressing Hen down. Any second, she expected to feel the fireball's impact. The high trill of Peter's flute filled the forest. Straight ahead of them, a giant fir split with a deafening crack. Izzy screamed as it fell toward them.

"We can make it!" shouted Selden. He put his head down and raced beneath the falling fir with Dree and Lug by his side.

Whoosh! Izzy's hair was blown forward as the tree fell right behind Selden into the path of Morvanna's missile. The fir exploded into white sparks. It crashed down onto the closest Unglers and blocked the others behind a fiery blaze.

The Changelings ran on, away from the light and the sap-fueled heat. Behind them, Izzy could hear Morvanna's angry cries echoing through the dark.

THE PURPLE MAN ON
THE MOUNTAIN

THE CHANGELINGS BOUNDED UP the mountain: a stag, a woolly ram with thick, curling horns, and a slender fawn whose hooves click-clacked over the stones. Izzy rode with her arms around Hen, clutching tight to the fur at Selden's neck. Up and up they cantered, until she felt like her teeth would shake loose from the jostling. She looked over her shoulder for the hundredth time, searching for the Unglers loping after them. But the woods held nothing except darkness and moonlight.

The Changelings held their pace until the ground became too steep. Selden stopped and bent down to let the girls slide off his back. He gave his sweat-drenched coat a shake before Changing back to himself.

"Whoa," said Hen.

Lug Changed back to his normal form, followed by Dree.

"Whoa…whoa…" Hen looked at Izzy and leaned back expectantly.

Izzy laughed. "Don't worry, I'm still me. Hen, these are the friends I was telling you about. They're Changelings, just like the ones in the stories I read you."

Selden and Dree shook Hen's hand. Lug picked her up and squeezed her in a hug.

Hen sniffed the top of his head. "You smell like Dublin."

"Is that a dessert?"

"No. He's my dog."

They all laughed, and the Changelings took turns congratulating themselves on their brilliant disguises.

Selden pointed to Lug. "And you! Even when you put on that goblin Likeness, you still kept the woman's bosom!"

"Well, it was such a good hiding place for pastries," said Lug.

"You both made very convincing goblins," said Dree. "I was completely disgusted by you."

"Izzy, you were great back there," said Selden. "Did you see Morvanna's face when you kicked her? She never saw that coming!"

The mention of Morvanna broke Izzy out of her reverie. "There's something I need to tell you."

The laughter faded, and the Changelings gathered closer around Izzy. She filled them in on everything—how she'd gotten lost and ended up outside Morvanna's tent. She told them about Peter, working with the Unglers to hunt Changelings on Earth, and about Morvanna learning about Yawning Top and the Scarlet Stairstep. Izzy paused, wondering how she was going to say what she had to tell them next.

"Morvanna talked about the other Changelings," she said. "I—I think I know what she did to them."

Everyone leaned in closer. Izzy looked down so she didn't have to see her friends' faces when she said it. "She's using their hearts to make a potion. It's how she gets her powers."

Lug put both hands over his chest. "Are you sure?"

Izzy nodded.

"But…their hearts?" said Dree. "That means they must be—"

"Dead," said Selden.

Izzy reached out for him, but he shrugged away from her.

Hen petted Lug's shoulder while he sobbed softly. "Oh, dear… All our friends…"

"What are you so upset about?" snapped Selden. "We wanted to find out what happened to them, didn't we? Now we know. We're the only ones left, so you better get used to it." Without waiting for a reply, he Changed into a wolf and trotted away from them, into the shadows.

Izzy started to go after him, but Dree held her back. "Just let him go," she whispered.

Lug blew his nose into his sleeve. "He doesn't mean it," he said as he sniffled. "He's just as torn up as we are."

Izzy slipped her hand into Dree's. "I'm sorry," she whispered.

A cold gust of wind blew down on them from above. Dree

wiped a tear from her cheek. She looked up at the gathering clouds and smelled the air.

"Knew it," she said softly. "It's going to rain."

Before continuing on, they dug a deep hole and buried their Scarlet Stairstep. Now that Morvanna knew their trick, the necklaces were useless at hiding them from the Unglers' well-trained snouts. Selden scouted ahead and found a faint track that continued up the mountain. A rockslide had almost completely hidden it from view. The rocks wouldn't cover their scent, but at least it would slow down their pursuers.

Once they climbed over the rockslide, they followed the trail as it switched back and forth across the face of the mountain. It was very narrow, more fit for goats than people. Dree followed Selden as a cat, with Lug walking behind as the fluffy ram. Izzy and Hen brought up the rear. Farther up, the trees thinned, and Izzy could make out the Apple Festival lanterns twinkling down below. As the track led them onto the northern side of Mount Mooring, the view of Avhalon and its rivers disappeared behind the shoulder of the mountain.

Between breaks in the clouds, the full moon shone so brightly that Izzy could have read a book by its light. When she looked over the edge of the track—which she tried not to do if she could help it—she saw the tiny silhouettes of fir trees, like the models from a train set. From the festival grounds, Mount

Mooring had seemed enormous, but now she could see much taller, white-capped peaks in the distance. Row upon row of mountains filled the horizon to the north and west.

"I wonder what lives out there," she said.

"That's the Norlorn Range," said Dree with a swish of her slinky tail. "Home to trolls and ice giants and wild, lawless sorts of fairies like the Wevildale goblins."

Izzy fell quiet again, wondering if there was any pocket of Faerie not full of danger. As the track led them through switchback after steep switchback, she thought of all the conditioning drills her old gym teacher forced her P.E. class to do. Completely useless. They should have been climbing up and down the school stairs with sacks of flour on their backs. As the track turned east, it became wider, which meant she didn't worry so much about falling off the side. But thick banks of clouds rolled over the moon, and the wind picked up sharply. Just when Izzy felt like her thighs couldn't handle another step, the ground started sloping downward. Although it wasn't as tiring as climbing up, she had to be careful not to slip on the loose gravel under her feet. Lightning flickered in the clouds overhead, followed by the slow rumble of thunder.

"All right, everyone, back to normal," said Selden, Changing back into himself. "I think we should hold hands for a while."

They inched along in the dark with their backs to the mountain. Izzy held on to Lug with one hand and Hen with the other. The wind blew harder and colder with every gust.

"Just a little farther," shouted Selden between thunderclaps. "We'll find a cave or an overhang and wait out the storm."

A shrill blast pressed them against the mountain wall. A scatter of fat raindrops hit Izzy's face.

"Here it comes!" shouted Dree.

All at once, the rain came down in solid, stinging sheets. When the wind blew, it drove the freezing drops sideways, pummeling them against the mountain wall. Within seconds, Izzy was soaked through every layer of clothing. Still, they all crept along the track, moving an inch at a time. Even when the lightning flashed, Izzy could see nothing but gray water and gray rock. Beneath their feet, the track had quickly become a river of mud.

Beside her, Hen stumbled. "My slipper! It fell off!"

"Hold on a second," Izzy shouted to Lug. She let go of his hand and bent down to feel the track at Hen's feet. "I can't find it! It must have fallen off the side. Come on. You'll just have to walk without it."

Izzy reached out for Lug again, but her hand touched air. Still gripping Hen, she took a step forward and blindly waved her other hand around in the darkness.

"Lug?" she cried. "Lug!"

"What is it?" shouted Hen.

"I've lost them!" Izzy peered through the rain, looking for a sign of the others, but she could barely even make out Hen just beside her.

"What do we do now?" cried Hen. "If it rains any harder, I'll drown!"

"Let's keep going," said Izzy. "They can't be too far ahead."

Izzy placed her hand back on the mountain and shuffled forward with her head down. Hen limped along behind her. They called Lug's name again and again, but only the wind roared back at them.

Suddenly, the track dropped. Izzy's feet flew out from underneath her. She fell onto her side, and Hen's hand slipped out of hers. She grasped for something to hold on to, but she was sliding too fast. Mud and gravel flew up and hit her in the face. She covered her eyes with one arm to protect them. Her shirt bunched up around her armpits. Her bare ribs and back scraped against the muddy ground. Twisting, she managed to roll onto her stomach. She dug her fingers and the toes of her boots into the ground until she slowed to a stop.

Izzy scrambled to her hands and knees and felt around for her sister.

"Hen? Hen!"

She swung her arms out in all directions, searching for the mountain wall, but it was gone.

"Izzy? Izzy?" It was Hen, calling her name from somewhere in the storm.

"Here! I'm here!" she shouted. A sharp gust of wind washed away her voice.

"Izzy? Where are you?" The voice grew fainter. Hen was moving away from her.

Izzy tried to stand up, but her clothes were plastered against her skin, weighing her down. On hands and knees, she forced herself to crawl over the gritty mud. Lightning pulsed, but she still couldn't get her bearings. What if she and Hen unknowingly crawled right off the side of the mountain? She opened her eyes wide against the blackness, willing them to see something, anything.

A cluster of hazy amber lights appeared in the distance.

Izzy kept her eyes on the haloed lights as she pressed through the rain. As she drew closer, one of the points of light moved away from the others. The light bobbed up and down like a firefly. It darted to the side and disappeared, then came back into view again. With a lurch in her stomach, Izzy worried it was a troll or one of the other wild mountain creatures Dree had mentioned. Her teeth chattered so hard she couldn't close her jaw, and her fingers had lost their feeling. She decided she didn't care what it was—troll or not—if she stayed put, she and Hen would die of hypothermia.

"Over here!" she shouted to the light. "Here!"

The light swung toward her and floated closer, growing in size. In a moment, it was almost on top of her. She realized it was the light from a lamp mounted onto a helmet. A huge purple head with two hideous, insect eyes loomed above her. Izzy shrieked and recoiled from the face. Gloved hands reached up and pulled the eyes down and off. In their place, the face of a young man with red cheeks stared down at her in surprise.

"Bless my bones," he said. "A child!"

TOM DIFFLEY

Rain drummed against the window. Izzy had been standing there for a half hour, even though she couldn't see anything in the glass but her own anxious reflection. Behind her, Hen sat on the edge of a stone fireplace, catching the tip of a stick on fire and blowing it out.

"You're going to get burned," said Izzy.

"You sound like Mom." Hen looked up at Izzy and smiled. "Hey, don't be so worried. That nice man will find them just like he found us."

Izzy wrapped herself tighter in the blanket the red-cheeked man had given her. The Changelings were tough, but even they couldn't survive outside on a night like this. She turned from the window and paced in front of the door.

Their rescuer had the strangest house Izzy had ever seen. The downstairs was one large room, with a ladder at the far end leading up to a second floor. Copper pipes and little brass wheels crisscrossed the ceiling, and every rug, curtain, and blanket in the room was a different shade of violet.

Izzy held out her eggplant-colored blanket, turning it over. "Don't you think it's weird that everything in this house is purple?"

"I guess fairies like colorful things," said Hen. "My room in Morvanna's castle was pink, floor to ceiling. I had a ginormous pink bed with pink satin pillows."

"Pink satin pillows?" Izzy couldn't help laughing. She thought of the nights she spent in Lug's bed of sticks or buried in itchy leaves. "The whole time I was looking for you, I thought you were in the bottom of some dark dungeon!"

"No way. I had toys and all the princess clothes I wanted, and if I needed anything, the guards had to get it for me."

Izzy sat down beside her sister at the fireplace. "But weren't you afraid? All by yourself in that castle with Morvanna and all those goblins?"

"I was at first," said Hen with a little shrug. "But they all pretty much left me alone. The only time I ever saw Morvanna was when she was getting Peter to make me laugh."

"So you know about that? Did you know she was stealing your laughter to make an elixir?"

"Yeah, but it didn't hurt, so I figured it was OK. If I would have known what else she was putting in that potion, I never would have laughed for her."

Izzy brushed a stray curl off Hen's forehead. "You're pretty brave, you know that?"

Hen smiled and poked her tongue through the gap in her teeth. "Thanks. But if it weren't for Peter, then I probably would have been scared."

"Peter?" asked Izzy, leaning back. "But he's the one who stole you in the first place! And he's Morvanna's servant."

"I know, but he was the only one who was nice to me. He did things to make me laugh even when Morvanna wasn't around."

Izzy shook her head at her sister. "Oh, Hen, you've always been so gullible."

Hen scrunched up her face and sat up taller. "I am not! If anyone tried to eat me, I'd punch them in the nose!"

"Not *edible*. Gullible. It means you always believe anything."

"Oh. Well, *you* always think you know everything."

Izzy turned away from the flames. "Not always," she whispered. For example, at this moment, she had absolutely no idea how they were ever going to get back home.

She was just about to go to the window and look for the others again, when the door banged open. Dree and Selden stood in the doorway, dripping wet and shivering. Izzy threw her blanket off her lap and jumped up.

"Thank goodness! What happened to you? Where's Lug?"

Selden put his finger to his lips and nodded behind him.

The red-cheeked man followed them in. "If you're talking about your ram, he's in the barn with my sheep," he said. He took off his goggles and headlamp and pulled off his muddy boots by the door.

Selden and Dree shuffled over to the fireplace, teeth chattering. Izzy wrapped her blanket around Dree's shoulders. She hoped the barn was warm for Lug's sake.

The man took off his gloves and hat and shook the water from his curly brown hair. When Izzy saw him on the mountain, he had looked so large and intimidating, but once he peeled off his thick purple coat, she saw how thin and wiry he really was. As far as she could tell, he seemed like a nice, though nervous, person. He lingered by the front door, like he might run out of it at any moment.

"Thank you so much for helping us," said Izzy. "Won't you tell us your name?"

"The name's—" His voice cracked. He cleared his throat and started again. "The name's Tom Diffley. And I don't have any treasure here, and I never disturbed a grave in my life."

"OK…" said Izzy. She looked at Dree and Selden, but they shook their heads, as confused as she was. "Tom, could we please have something to drink? Something hot, maybe?"

"I'll boil a kettle," said Tom. He backed up all the way to his tiny kitchen. "I guess you want real water in it?"

"Um, yeah, that would be great," said Izzy. She leaned over to Hen. "Is it just me, or is this guy a little weird?"

"He looks like he's about to throw up," whispered Hen.

In the kitchen, Tom pulled a wooden lever on the wall. Water trickled through the pipes overhead into a kettle suspended from a cable. When the kettle was full, the weight of it sent it wheeling along the cable like a zip line, where it stopped just over the fire. Tom went to the wall beside the fireplace and pulled down on a series of ropes. Above them, a flat plank of wood lowered down until it stopped at table height. Tom brought over four chairs and sat them at the table, then set out some cups and saucers. His hands shook as he poured the kettle, spilling steaming water onto the table.

Tom raised his cup to his lips, eyeing them over the rim. It took him a moment to realize the cup didn't have anything in it.

"Tom, is anything wrong?" asked Izzy.

He set his cup down and backed away. "Now listen, if you're all shades, then just come right out and say it!"

"Shades?" asked Izzy.

"Ghosts! Of folks who've died in the mountains! Why else would you be out wandering in this storm? One of you is clear as glass!" He nodded at Dree, who hid her bare arms behind her back. "And you," he said, sweeping his hand to Selden. "You popped up out of the shadows, out of nowhere. Just like a ghost!"

Selden rubbed the back of his neck guiltily. Izzy guessed Tom must have caught him in the middle of a Change.

"I'm sure it was just the storm playing tricks on your eyes," she said.

"Are your ears a trick?" asked Tom, pointing at her, then Hen. "There's been no human children in Eidenloam Valley for fifty years. You've got to be specters!" He took a few steps backward toward the ladder. "Listen, I'm dead tired, and I want to go to bed. But I can't sleep knowing there's shades sitting around my table. So if you are ghosts, then just get on out the door and go back to where you came from."

"We're not ghosts, I promise," said Izzy.

"Yeah," said Hen. "See, we're sisters, and they're—ow!" She scowled at Dree. "Hey—you pinched me!"

"He doesn't need to know everything about us!" Dree hissed.

"Oh, come on. You can't be serious," said Izzy. "He saved all our lives out there. Maybe he can help us."

"Yeah," said Hen. "And if Morvanna's chasing us, he needs to know what he's getting into."

Dree smacked her palm to her forehead.

At the mention of Morvanna, Tom went green. "No, no," he said, holding up both hands. He took another step backward. "I don't need to know. Nothing'll come of it but me getting into trouble, and I'd just as soon stay ignorant, if you don't mind. Long as you're not shades, you can all stay till the storm clears, then be off on your way."

The front door slammed open. Lug stood in the doorway with his arms wrapped around himself, shivering violently.

"C-c-can't s-s-stay out there any l-l-longer," he said. "Th-th-those sheep s-s-smell, and one of 'em b-b-bit me in the b-b-backside!"

Tom's eyes bulged. "What in the name of—" He stopped

and held his hands up again. "No, I don't want to know. Truly, just keep it to yourselves!"

Once they all dried off, Tom showed them upstairs to their rooms.

"This was my pa's room when he was still alive," he said, holding a door open for Izzy and Hen. He pulled a lever on the wall next to the door, and a panel in the floor slid open. With the turn of a wheel, a bed rose up from the planks. "I built this for him when he got older so he could get in and out of bed easy."

"Can I ask you something?" said Izzy. "You say you're a sheep farmer, but you seem more like an inventor to me."

Tom brightened and puffed out his thin chest. "That's right. But all this stuff in the house is nothing to what I've got out in the barn. I'll show you tomorrow, if it ever stops raining."

A small bookshelf stood against the far wall of the room. Izzy's fingers itched to open one of the books. It felt like such a long time since she'd even held one. "Is it all right if I look through those later?" she asked.

"Fine with me," said Tom, rummaging through a trunk filled with purple clothes. "Here, these should do for night things." He tossed some old flannel shirts and wool socks onto the bed. "I'm turning in. See you in the morning." On his way out of the room, he stopped in front of Izzy. He closed one eye, and pressed a finger down onto the top of her head.

"I'm *not* a ghost," she said with a laugh.

"Doesn't hurt to check. All right, girls, good night!"

Izzy and Hen dressed themselves head to toe in violet. Outside, the wind had stopped screaming, and the rain beat out a steady rhythm against the window. Hen jumped onto the bed and burrowed under the covers.

"I'll be right back," said Izzy. "I just have to check something."

She went down the hallway to the Changelings' room. She peeked around the doorway. Selden sat next to Lug at the foot of a small bed, his head in his hands. Lug had one arm over his friend's shoulder, talking to him in a low, gentle voice. Dree stood in the corner. When she saw Izzy, she tiptoed out into the hallway.

"Is Selden OK?" whispered Izzy.

"He'll be all right," said Dree, shutting the door behind her. "He just needs a little time, that's all."

"It's what I said, isn't it? About Morvanna and what she did to your friends."

"It isn't your fault," said Dree. She led Izzy farther into the dark hall. "Listen, I think there's something you should know about Selden."

"OK. What is it?"

"Did you know that the three of us were all on Earth when Morvanna first showed up in Avhalon?" Dree whispered.

Izzy nodded. "Selden told me that when we were at the Giant's Boneyard."

"Well, Selden should have been here in Faerie. It wasn't his turn to do the Exchange, but he didn't want to wait. He's always so impatient. He tricked Peter into letting him go first. When Morvanna became queen and the Changelings disappeared, Selden should have been with them. But he wasn't. He was on Earth."

"But it's not his fault that Morvanna captured the other Changelings," said Izzy.

"He thinks if he had been here, he could have fought her, that he could have saved the others."

"But that's crazy," said Izzy. "He would just have been caught too. He shouldn't blame himself."

"You've got no idea how many times I've told him the exact same thing," said Dree. She leaned back against the wall. In the dim light, her skin shimmered like the raindrops streaming down the window. "Izzy, have you ever been pricked by a devil's hackbush? It's got these barbed thorns, and once they get in your skin, you can't pull them back out. You just have to wait for them to work themselves out through the other side. Well, Selden's the type who won't leave something like that alone. He keeps picking at it, and now the wound is big and raw."

No wonder Selden had such a dark cloud hanging over him. Now he would never have the chance to tell his friends he was sorry. He'd never get the chance to make things right.

The floorboards creaked, and Lug leaned out into the hallway. "He's asleep," he whispered. "You coming, Dree?"

Before she left, Dree turned back to Izzy. "You won't tell a soul any of that, will you?" she whispered.

Izzy held up three fingers of her right hand. "Spy's honor."

A FAIRY LIBRARY

TOM DIFFLEY WAS SO kind and so patient and cooked
such good fried eggs and biscuits that by the end of breakfast
the next day, they trusted him enough to tell him everything
about themselves. Even Dree let down her guard and helped
recount their adventures, while Tom muttered, "My bones,
my bones…" through the entire tale.

The rain didn't let up that morning or the next, trapping
them all inside for three days. The only good thing about
it was knowing the Unglers wouldn't be able to track them.
They spent the hours dozing, eating, and playing card games
that Izzy and Hen had never heard of before. In the evenings,
Hen and Dree would dress up in swaths of purple cloth and
act out fairy tales that Izzy narrated from memory, while the
others drank hot tea and played the part of the audience. The
Changelings found the happy endings hilariously unlikely.

Selden had spent the first two days staring blankly out the

window, but criticizing Izzy's stories seemed to cheer him up. "Don't these princes have anything better to do than wander around the woods looking for girls to kiss? Who's watching over their kingdoms? And what kind of fool names their child Snow White, anyway?"

"Tell us the one about the mermaid again," said Dree, wrapping her legs up in an indigo sheet. "That one's so heartbreaking, it must be real."

This went on late into the night, until Hen fell asleep by the fire, and Lug had to carry her upstairs with everyone else yawning and dragging themselves up behind them.

On the third day, the rain gave way to a light drizzle, and Tom offered to take them out to have a look at his invention. Izzy made up an excuse, wanting to stay behind so she could finally look through the books in his father's room. These weren't books *about* fairies; they were books written *by* fairies. But a first glance over the titles proved disappointing. *A General Historie of Hued Sheep Breeding* and *The Cultivation of Violet Milkwort* were not exactly the thrilling subjects she'd had in mind. She was just about to pull one down from its shelf when Selden popped his head into the room.

"Can I have a look?" he asked, walking to the bookshelf.

"Are you sure? I didn't think you were a fan of books."

Selden cracked a smile. "Not human books, of course. But if you're nice, I'll let you read me one of these."

Izzy smiled back. "Ooh, lucky me."

Right beside *From Toadstool to Stump: A Catalogue of Gnome Architecture*, a tall book caught her eye. The gold letters on the cover read, *The Old Tales, Illustrated*. She carefully opened the crumbling cover. Each page held a single ink drawing, with the title written on the facing page.

"Yeah, that one," said Selden. "It's got lots of pictures."

"You sound just like Hen."

Izzy gently flipped through the brittle pages. The illustrations were beautiful: flying dragons, a girl with an apple tree growing out of her hair, a bear hatching out of an egg. Selden sat beside her on the floor and told her the stories behind all the drawings. They were just like fairy tales from her books back home, but these stories were bloodier and sad, and according to Selden, completely true. With every tale, he became more and more talkative and started making jokes, comparing the characters to the ones from Izzy's fairy tales.

"Come on, you've got to admit our stories are better," he said. "Your princesses are always fainting or falling asleep. Ours know how to gut a troll with a knitting needle."

Izzy held her tongue. By now, she knew Selden well enough to know that teasing was his way of making conversation. Besides, it was nice to see him smiling again.

Izzy turned the page to a picture of a king and a farmer clasping hands. "Hey, I've seen this before!" she said. "At Netherbee Hall, this was carved into the courtyard door. And inside the house, there was an old painting of the same picture. The title here says it's *King Revelrun and Master Green*."

"Oh sure, you find those carvings all over the place around Netherbee," said Selden. "It's because all the paths that lead to Earth start in the Edgewood. Revelrun was the one who did the magic that split up our worlds. Supposedly, he said humans wouldn't know a good thing if they were stepping right on it. That's why he put Faerie underground, kind of as a joke."

"They seem like good friends to me," said Izzy. "Look, they're smiling and shaking hands."

"They're probably happy they're going to stay out of each other's business."

Izzy leaned back and looked at Selden. "There are so many stories. How do you know them all?"

"Good Peter told them to us when we were growing up. He knows every story there is." Selden flipped the pages until he landed on an illustration of a man playing a flute, surrounded by animals sitting at his feet. Just like at Netherbee Hall, the animals all had children's faces. "That's him, the Piper."

"But I don't understand," said Izzy. "All of these drawings are supposed to be old. When I saw Good Peter, he looked so young."

"He's a Neverborn," said Selden. When Izzy still looked confused, he rolled his eyes. "Don't they teach you anything useful up there? You know, like the North Wind? Or Father

Christmas? They've been around since the beginning. The *very* beginning."

"Gosh, I wish Father Christmas was the one who kidnapped Hen," said Izzy. "I could be sitting at the North Pole right now, drinking hot chocolate and feeding the reindeer." She smiled, but Selden didn't laugh. That gloomy cloud had gathered over his face again.

"I'm sorry about Peter," she said. "What he did to your friends was a real betrayal."

Selden shook his head. "I just don't understand why he'd do it. He was never very warm or loving or anything like that. But I still felt like he cared about us. Shank always likes to say that everyone has their price. I guess Morvanna knew Peter's."

They sat in silence for a while. Outside, the rain had slowed to a drizzle, which meant they would all be leaving in the morning. Tom had offered to take them east through the Avhal Mountains, all the way to the Edgewood, and then help the girls look for their way back home. The Changelings would strike out by themselves for the deep woods, far from the City Road, far from anyone.

"I wish you three would come with us instead," said Izzy.

Selden pushed the book off his knee onto Izzy's lap. "No, you're better off without us around so you won't have to worry about the Unglers. Besides, what would your parents say if you showed up with the three of us? They'd probably make us go to school." He smiled. "Think I'd rather take my chances in the Edgewood."

Izzy shut the book and reached out to set it back in its place, when a thundering *boom!* shook the floor and rattled the windows of the room. Selden and Izzy both grabbed onto the bookshelf to keep it from falling over on top of them. Once the vibrations stopped, they hurried to the window that looked out onto the barn.

"What in the world…"

Another boom sounded. This time, a large, hairy figure launched into the air, its arms flailing about as it sailed through the sky.

"That was Lug," said Selden. "Come on!"

Izzy rushed after him down the stairs and out the back door. The barn was uphill, between Tom's house and the mountain peak. A mucky field lay between the two buildings. Izzy's boots squelched through the mud as she followed Selden to a lumpy mound in the center of the field.

"Lug! Are you all right?" called Selden, sliding onto his knees in the mud.

The mound sat up and spat a glob of brown ooze out of its mouth.

"I've died, haven't I?" said Lug. "I always knew the afterlife would look like this."

Selden gave him a punch on the shoulder. "Lug, you lump! I thought you were in trouble!"

"Sorry! Sorry!" called Tom. He ran down from the barn with Dree and Hen at his heels. Behind them waddled a flock of fat, woolly sheep. Now Izzy understood Tom's strange color obsession. Each one of his sheep was a different shade of vibrant purple.

"That was awesome!" said Hen, throwing her arms around Lug's neck. "You definitely went higher than the house!"

"Sorry again," said Tom. "Didn't mean to launch you so high. I'm still working on how much blitzing powder to use in the catapult."

Hen's face and hands were covered in a thin film of black dust. She had that look of sheer joy she only got during fireworks shows. "Just a little more blitzing powder, and I bet you could launch a wool bale into the next village," she said.

"And crush a house while you're at it!" said Selden.

An enormous wooden catapult stood in the shade of the barn. "*That's* your invention?" asked Izzy.

"It needs some adjusting, as you can see," said Tom, scratching the back of his head. "But once I get the right ratio for the powder, it'll cut wool transport time down to nothing."

Lug dug his finger in his tufted ears and excavated a plug of mud. "If you can't get it to work for wool, you should sell tickets for it. But not for me. I think I much prefer staying on the ground." One of the purple sheep licked his cheek. He pushed it off. "Away from me, you bottom-biter!"

The sheep turned and waddled indignantly down the hill toward the green valley below.

Tom whistled for them, but they only trotted away faster. He called again. "Now what in Faerie's got into them?"

The drizzle had stopped, and the air was still and quiet except for the tinkling of the sheep's bells. A tickly feeling inched up the back of Izzy's neck. She turned around and looked up. High above, tiny flecks of black circled the peak of Mount Mooring.

"Izzy? What is it?" asked Dree, following her gaze.

"I was looking up there, at those birds," she answered, pointing to the mountain. Something about their slow wheeling made her uneasy.

One of the birds peeled away from the others. It dropped down from the peak and headed toward them.

Tom put his hands on Hen's shoulders and turned her toward the house. "Maybe we better get back inside."

Before anyone could answer, the air screamed with the force of flapping wings. They all ducked to the ground. The giant bird swooped low overhead. It wasn't a bird at all but a serpent with jagged teeth and scales the color of ashes.

A goblin rode perched between its leathery wings.

NETS OF SILVER

Tom's face went white. "Wyverns!"

"Wy-what?" said Hen.

"Like dragons, but smaller," said Dree.

"And faster, and fiercer!" cried Lug. "What do we do?"

"Get to the barn!" called Tom, already pulling Hen in that direction.

Izzy's boots caught in the mud as she tried to run after Tom and her sister. In the sky overhead, the goblin who'd ridden past them snapped the wyvern's flanks with his whip. The beast pulled up and turned around to dive on them again.

The barn seemed miles away, and there was nowhere to hide on the open field. The other wyverns flying over Mount Mooring joined the first and circled over them. A second wyvern dove down, so close that Izzy could see the gleam of the metal bit clamped between its teeth.

As it passed over, its goblin shouted a command. The

wyvern released a shimmering object from its talons that unfurled as it fell.

"Lug, watch out!" shouted Izzy.

Lug covered his head as the silver net fell over him. Leather weights at the net's corners whipped around his legs. Lug struggled beneath the net, changing frantically from one form to another. The wyvern flew down again, talons bared to scoop him up, net and all.

A wolf's howl rang off the mountainside. Selden ran to Lug, snapping his jaws at the wyvern's foot. The beast dodged him and rose back into the air.

"They need help!" cried Izzy.

Tom grabbed her arm before she could run to them. "Not like that," he shouted, pulling Hen and Izzy behind him toward the barn. "Come on. Dree's got the better idea!"

In the sky, Dree was the scissor-tailed bird, dive-bombing their attackers. When one of the goblins drove his wyvern down at Selden, she flapped in his face and clawed at his eyes. He pulled the beast back, lost his balance, and slipped off his saddle. The goblin held tight to the wyvern's reins, yanking its head forward. It flapped its wings, but it couldn't manage to pull its head up. The beast twirled downward and crashed to the ground with a wet thud. The wyvern got to its feet and limped away, leaving its goblin rolling in the muck.

While Selden and Dree continued to hold the other wyverns off Lug, Tom and the girls reached the barn.

Tom put his shoulder against his catapult. "Come on! Help me swing this thing around!"

The wheels creaked as Izzy and Hen helped him swivel the catapult to face the Changelings. The machine was a web of wooden linkages, gears, and cables. At the top, a huge wooden bowl was bolted to the end of a long lever arm. Tom grabbed a bale of wool and chucked it up into the bowl.

"Just like I showed you, Hen," he said, cranking a handle. "Tamp it down tight!"

Hen was already quick at work, packing a wad of blitzing powder into a receptacle at the base of the machine. She gave it a final tamp, then held up her thumb. "Loaded and ready!"

Tom shoved a box of matches into Izzy's hand. "Get one ready, but don't light the tinder till I say."

Izzy struck the match and held it over the powder box.

Tom squinted up at the wyverns. He adjusted the catapult's lever arm. "Hold on...not yet...now!"

Izzy let her match fall onto the blitzing powder. It fizzed and crackled. The catapult lurched backward with a boom that shook the ground and knocked her over. A mass of dark purple hurtled up through the air. The wool bale slammed into one of the beasts, sending it tumbling in a chaotic spiral to the ground.

Izzy leapt to her feet. "Yes! We got him!"

"Four to go!" shouted Hen.

Tom swiveled the machine to the left. He reloaded as Hen

packed in another round of powder and Izzy lit her match. That bale veered wide of its target, but their next shot knocked a goblin down from his mount. Without a rider, the wyvern seemed to lose direction and flew shrieking back toward the mountain peak.

On the ground, Selden was all teeth and claws, snapping at anything that dared fly too low. Between him and Dree and the catapult, the remaining wyverns couldn't get close enough to grab Lug.

Tom and the girls fired another shot. This time, their target saw it coming. The goblin yanked his wyvern's reins, and the beast dodged out of the way. It followed the wool bale on its descent and snatched it up in its talons. With a pump of its wings, it turned, its eyes trained on the catapult.

"Hurry, load it again!" shouted Izzy.

"Oh no." Hen looked up with a face caked in soot. "We're out of blitzing powder!"

"I've got more in the kitchen," said Tom. "Come on, quick!"

They sprinted toward Tom's house. When they were halfway across the field, the wyvern dropped the wool bale onto the catapult. The machine exploded into splinters. The goblin shouted triumphantly and turned his beast at the girls.

Tom grabbed a long plank thrown from the crushed catapult. "You girls go on to the house!" He ran back toward the barn, waving the plank overhead like a baseball bat. "Hey, down here, you lizards!"

While Tom drew attention away from them, Izzy and Hen raced for the front porch. Out on the field, two goblins who'd been knocked off their wyverns had recovered and were approaching Lug on foot. Selden backed up against him.

"Just leave me!" pleaded Lug. "I'm done for. Just go!"

Selden snapped and growled at the goblins as they closed in around him. One goblin rushed forward. When Selden turned to strike, the other goblin pulled a club from his belt and pummeled Selden on the back of the head. Selden sank to the ground. In a flash of silver, Dree was beside him. She Changed back to her normal self and kneeled over him, shielding him with her thin arms. With loud squawks, the wyverns dropped nets over both of them.

The goblin with the club turned away from the netted Changelings. He spotted the girls and broke into a malicious grin.

Izzy pulled her sister up Tom's porch steps. "Hurry, Hen, hurry!"

She pushed Hen inside the house, slammed the door, and slid a chair in front of it. In Tom's kitchen, she yanked open the bottom cabinets until she found an empty one.

"Quick, get in," she told Hen.

"But what about you?"

Izzy crammed her sister into the cupboard. "Shhh!"

The front door rattled. "Open up! I see you in there!" barked a goblin's voice. The door shuddered with the force of his club.

Izzy searched the room. She found what she was looking for: a burlap sack on the counter. She grabbed the sack, ripped it open, and scattered its contents on the floor in front of her. Breathless, she stood at the kitchen threshold, waiting.

The front door split with a crack. The goblin reached inside and shoved the chair out of the way. He swung open the shattered door and stepped into the house. Izzy recognized him as the guard who'd left Hen to get her a fried apple tart back at the festival. Where his long, pointed nose had been there was now just a charred, oozing stump.

The goblin chattered his teeth excitedly as he stepped toward Izzy. "I know she's here, that lyin' little brat. Now we'll see who's a little princess, won't we? It's her I've got to thank for this." He pointed at his ruined nose.

Izzy guessed Morvanna must have punished him for leaving his post. She gulped and took one step back. "Don't come any closer, or you'll be sorry."

The goblin laughed. He tramped forward. "I will, huh? And what's a little speck like you gonna do to me? I could squash you under my boot, and nobody'd notice you're gone."

Izzy backed up a little more. She stopped once the goblin set foot into the kitchen. "Speaking of boots," she said. "Maybe you should watch where you step."

The goblin looked down. His yellow eyes widened when he saw that he stood in the middle of a scattered pile of black powder.

Izzy took Tom's matches from her pocket. She struck one against the matchbox and held it out in front of her. "One more step, and I'll drop it."

The goblin released his nasty grin. "You won't..."

Izzy set her jaw. "Oh, won't I? You've got no idea what crazy things we humans will do."

Another goblin appeared in the doorway. When he saw Izzy, the match, and the powder, he backed away. "Just leave 'em be!" he shouted. "We got the Changelings! The queen can always find more human brats if she wants 'em!"

The charred-nose goblin snarled at Izzy. His body twitched like he might rush at her. He glanced at the burning match. Then he spat on the floor at her feet, turned, and tromped out the door.

Izzy held the match up to her lips. Her breath was so shaky, it took her a few tries to blow it out. Behind her, the cabinet door swung open, and Hen climbed out. She ran to Izzy and hugged her around the waist.

"It's all right. We're OK," said Izzy, as much to reassure herself as her sister.

They looked up to see Tom leaning on the doorway. His clothes were ripped, and he held a bleeding cut on his shoulder. "I'm sorry...I couldn't stop them."

Izzy rushed to the window and pulled back the curtain. Three wyverns had landed on the field so the remaining goblins could climb onto their backs. The scaly beasts beat their wings and rose to the sky, each carrying a netted Changeling back toward the peak of Mount Mooring.

Izzy bolted for the front door.

Tom grabbed her elbow before she could get outside. "Get back here! They just let us be—you want them to change their minds?"

"Let go! I'm going after them!"

Tom pulled her back. "The other side of Mount Mooring is going to be thick with goblins. You try and go that way, and you'll get caught, no question."

"But we can't just abandon them! Morvanna will cut out their—she'll cut their—" Izzy couldn't say the words. She felt like something had its claws around her own heart.

"I didn't say we were abandoning them. I just said you can't go back to Avhalon the way you came, that's all."

"What do you mean?"

Tom sighed and shook his head. "I'm going to regret ever mentioning this, I just know it."

Izzy clasped her hands in front of her. "Tom, are you saying you know another way to get to Avhalon? Please tell me you do!"

Tom glanced at the windows like the goblins might hear him even now. He lowered his voice. "A long time ago, farmers down in the valley needed a way to get their animals to market in Avhalon. You think those sheep are gonna march their woolly butts over the top of Mount Mooring? There's a tunnel. It goes right under the mountain, straight to Avhalon. It's all but forgotten about nowadays. No one's used it for as long as I've been alive."

Izzy let his words sink in. "Under the mountain..."

Tom nodded slowly. "Takes you right to the banks of the Liadan River."

"But then how do we get inside once we're there?"

"There's a way to do that too," Tom whispered. "And I guarantee nobody but me knows about it."

Izzy's stomach did nervous, happy little flips. "We have to go right away! The wyverns are probably already back by now!"

"I'm ready!" piped up Hen.

Izzy turned. She'd almost forgotten her sister was even there. "You're not coming. You're staying right here where it's safe."

"What? I can't stay here. Mom and Dad say I'm not allowed to stay home by myself!"

"Oh, and you think Mom and Dad would *allow* you to go to a castle full of goblins and Unglers and who knows what else? You're not going, and if you try and follow me, I'm going to tie you to a chair!"

Hen squinted one eye and leaned forward. "Just try it."

"Hey, hey," said Tom, stepping between them.

Hen leaned around him and pointed at Izzy. "Don't boss me about being safe. You're always doing dangerous stuff. If you would have dropped that match, the whole house would have blown up—with us in it!"

Tom patted Hen's shoulder. "No, it wouldn't," he said calmly. He picked up the ripped burlap sack off the floor and showed it to Hen. The front was stamped with the words, *Genuine Coffee, Fine Ground.* "Your sister's clever, that's for sure. She's got a good head on her shoulders, and she's only looking after you…"

Izzy folded her arms and nodded.

"…but she's not right all the time."

"Ha!" said Hen.

Tom turned to Izzy. "This house isn't safe now that Morvanna knows you're here. The goblins were fine to leave you this time, but I bet she'll send them right back here to scoop you two up. They might already be on their way."

"Yeah," said Hen in her I-told-you-so voice. "Besides, if we're going to rescue the Changelings, then you have to take me with you. I'm the only one who's been inside the castle before."

"She's got a point there," said Tom.

Izzy fought the urge to grab her sister and shake her. She'd come all this way, rescued Hen against crazy odds, and now she was taking her right back to Avhalon, right back to Morvanna. It sounded like the most stupid idea she could think of. But there was no way around it. Either they leave the Changelings to die, or they all went in search of them together.

"Fine," said Izzy. She summoned up the decisive voice their mom used with them. "But you have to listen to me. No running off and doing your own thing. And no whining! Understand?"

Hen clicked her heels together and saluted. "Aye, aye, captain!"

Tom sighed and surveyed his ruined house. "Three days ago, I was a simple sheep farmer, minding my own business. Now I'm about to lead two humans through the Eidenloam Tunnel. If Pa was here, he'd say I've lost my ever-lovin' mind."

THE EIDENLOAM TUNNEL

IZZY SHOULD HAVE KNOWN that not whining was a promise her sister would never be able to keep.

"This sweater is so itchy!"

Hen tugged at the collar of the purple cardigan Tom had given her. She also wore wool pants cinched tight at the waist and a pair of Tom's house shoes with thick wool socks to make them fit better. She looked like a giant fluffy raisin. Izzy would have laughed, except she didn't look much better.

"I don't understand why we can't just wear our own clothes," grumbled Hen.

"You'll thank me once we're under the mountain," said Tom. He switched his rucksack to the other shoulder, rattling the equipment he had packed inside. "Where we're going, it's cold and wet, and that wool is going to keep you warm and dry."

The storm had dragged all the remaining summer away behind it, and the cold mountain air was sharp in Izzy's nostrils. Just like Hen, she carried all her regular clothes in a wool bag. They were hiking downhill, farther into the deep bowl of Eidenloam Valley. Below them, ribbons of smoke rose up from the chimneys of the small villages of the Eidenloam.

It almost hurt to look at the pretty little valley. If the wyverns hadn't shown up, they'd be walking down there right now, with the Changelings beside them, heading back to the Edgewood, back toward home. Instead, home was farther away than ever.

At noon, they stopped to eat some biscuits and cheese Tom had packed. When they finished, Tom led them off the trail, through a lush pasture of violet milkwort—the delicate flowers his sheep grazed on. They climbed down a rocky hill until they reached a stand of laurel trees growing against the mountain. They ducked beneath the smooth branches as they moved forward through the laurel. Tom pushed aside a cluster of saplings to reveal a dark opening in the mountain wall. A symbol was carved above the entrance: two hands, clasped at the wrists.

Hen tugged Izzy's sleeve and pointed at the ground. "Hey, look at that." A stack of five large stones stood on either side of the entrance. "Those are just like the ones we saw at Marian's house!"

"They're a sign of friendship between our worlds," said Tom. "Stone for Earth, leaf for Faerie. You used to see them all over the valley." He hung back from the opening. "There it is," he said, pointing into the darkness. "The Eidenloam Tunnel. In Pa's time, there was so much traffic between here and Avhalon, you had to get a ticket to go through. But now, it's empty."

"Why?" asked Hen, ducking under a laurel branch to get a better look. "Is it haunted or something?"

Izzy elbowed her in the back.

"Don't mention shades!" said Tom with a shudder. "It's bad enough we've got to go through there without imagining all the terrible ghosts we might meet!"

Good one, Izzy mouthed to Hen.

"Tom, you can't be scared now," said Hen. "We just battled a bunch of goblins riding on wyverns!"

"That's different. There wasn't time to think about it. And besides, the goblins were alive. Shades are—well, they're *shades*."

"*I'm* not scared of ghosts," said Hen, taking a step into the tunnel.

Izzy grabbed her by the back of the collar. "No, but you should be scared of whatever other creatures Morvanna has working for her. Tom, won't she be watching this tunnel?"

Tom shook his head. "I bet she doesn't even know it's here. She's come into the valley before, but every time, she's sent the wyverns up over the mountain. She wouldn't waste all that effort if she knew about this tunnel."

"All right," said Izzy. She grabbed Tom's shirtsleeve and pulled him along behind her. "Either we wait around for wyverns to spot us, or we take a chance with the ghosts. Personally, I'd rather meet the shades."

"Easy to say in the daylight," Tom said with a gulp, but he followed after her anyway.

Inside, the tunnel walls were slick with some kind of algae that gave off a faint phosphorescent glow. Otherwise, it was dark as midnight. Tom lit his headlamp. The beam cut through the darkness and illuminated a path that wound ahead into the black.

"OK," said Izzy, her whisper echoing softly off the damp walls. "Now or never."

She quickly realized she would have to go first if they were ever going to make any progress. Hen walked behind with Tom, holding his hand. The tunnel became colder the deeper they went. They walked a stone path worn smooth from heavy use and lined with deep wheel ruts. At times, the tunnel opened up to great rooms that extended beyond the reach of Tom's headlamp. The rooms glittered with stalactites that dripped watery melodies in the darkness.

Tom kept stopping and curling up with his arms around his knees. Not only had Hen put the fear of ghosts into him, but it turned out he was also claustrophobic. To keep him from dwelling on "being crushed under a million pounds of stone," Izzy tried to keep him talking.

"Tell us more about when your father was alive," she said. "Were there really that many fairies traveling through here?"

"There were," said Tom. "Eidenloam folk came this way to take their sheep and other goods to market in Avhalon. And the Avhalonians traveled in the other direction to consult with the humans."

"You mean they came this way to go to Earth?"

"Some. You can get to the Edgewood from here, but it's a long trip. Mostly they came to our villages to learn from the humans who lived there."

"Humans lived in Eidenloam Valley?" asked Hen.

"Lots of them." Tom's voice had stopped trembling, and he talked more easily now. "The Eidenloam was a human settlement hundreds of years ago. Back then, the valley was home to the best farmers, the best ranchers—"

"—the best inventors," said Izzy.

"That's right!" chuckled Tom. "Any human trade there was, Eidenloam had it."

Izzy stopped and turned around. "Wait a minute. Tom, are you part human?"

"You couldn't tell?" Tom smoothed his hair away from his ears. For the first time, Izzy noticed they were pointed but much rounder than the Changelings'. "Having human blood may not be fashionable nowadays, but we in the valley have always been proud of it. Makes us what we are."

They pressed on through the dark, with Tom telling Izzy about his lineage and the part-human, part-fairy villagers he grew up with in Eidenloam Valley. He explained that although humans didn't have magic powers, they had plenty of skills that didn't come naturally to fairies—logic, hardworking spirit, a desire to learn new things. The way Tom saw it, Faerie needed those qualities just as much as it needed pollenings and pixie dust.

Izzy began to see all her familiar stories in a new light: Cinderella's fairy godmother had plucked her pumpkin from the tidy rows of a human gardener. Rumpelstiltskin wove straw into gold on a human-made spinning wheel. Even Avhalon's famous apple trees would have stopped bearing fruit long ago if it weren't for human farmers who passed their knowledge down to their fairy cousins. Now Izzy understood that humans and fairies were part of the same story and had been for thousands of years. The Exchange might be keeping the two worlds connected, but even without it, Faerie and Earth were tied together.

"We've been walking for*ever*," said Hen with a groan.

"Can't be far now," said Tom.

"Now will you tell us your secret way into the castle?" asked Izzy.

"Pa told me all about it. I told you Morvanna sent wyverns over the mountain years ago to fetch some valley folk, didn't I? Well, my pa was one of them she took. It was back when she first started building her castle. She had big plans for it, but there's not many fairies in Avhalon that know how to build anything taller than a fruitcake."

Izzy nodded, thinking about all the tilted, ramshackle buildings she had seen in the city.

"So she came to the valley to get 'volunteers,'" Tom continued. "Slaves more like it. Pa was put in charge of the waterworks. The queen worked him down to the bone. He came back home but died that same winter."

"I'm so sorry," said Izzy.

Tom cleared his throat, and when he spoke again, his voice didn't shake at all. "I thought I could lay low in the valley, be a simple farmer, and forget all about Morvanna. But now I see that she aims to ruin everything she touches. Maybe if we can rescue the Bretabairn, we can finally put a stop to her."

If there were any ghosts beneath Mount Mooring, they kept to themselves. The sound of dripping water had grown steadily louder throughout their journey. Now, the little subterranean streams joined up with each other and sloshed over the tunnel trail.

"It's from all that rain we got," said Tom. "This mountain's as holey as a dragon-breeder's trousers."

Hen stamped through the water, splashing Izzy in the back. "This is so cool—my feet aren't even wet!"

"Told you that wool would keep you dry," said Tom. "My sheep are the very best."

A faint, liquid light shimmered up ahead, and the sound of rushing water grew to a roar. Tom explained that the tunnel exit was hidden behind a waterfall. They carefully followed the slippery trail out from behind the cascade. Izzy blinked in the too-bright light. It took her a moment to realize it was only the moon. They had hiked the entire day away. She suddenly felt exhausted, but there was no time to rest.

Tom pointed at the waterfall behind them. "This feeds into the Liadan River. We're close to Avhalon now."

Izzy took a breath and let her lungs fill with the scent of pine sap. They were back in the evergreen forest but on the eastern side of the river this time. Tom and the girls picked their way around the trees, staying close to the swollen river. When they were still fifty yards upstream from the Liadan Bridge, they crouched in the ferns on the riverbank. Avhalon's ancient city walls cast deep shadows over the dark water.

Being so close to Avhalon again put Izzy's whole body on edge. She listened for the sounds of Unglers shrieking or goblins shouting.

Tom pointed across the river. "You see that hole in the stone?" he whispered. "Look close, right at the waterline. That's our way in."

The circular hole was barely visible above the rushing water. A grate of vertical bars covered the dark opening.

Tom swung his bag off his shoulder and started digging through it. "That was Pa's project when he worked for the queen. All the other city folk haul their water out of the Liadan in buckets, but that wasn't good enough for Morvanna. She wanted it piped into the castle directly. Pa designed the whole thing. Water rushes in through that opening and flows under the city to the castle pump room. From there, it's piped all through the castle." He reached down into the bottom of his bag. "Now where'd I put that thing?"

Out in the middle of the river, a broken branch floated quickly past. Izzy was a decent swimmer, but she didn't know if she'd be able to make it across by herself. The current would definitely sweep Hen away.

"Tom, I don't know if this is going to work..."

"Now, don't give up till you hear me out." He dumped his bag out onto the grass. Ropes, pulleys, and half a dozen small wooden contraptions tumbled out. "Ha, knew I packed it!"

He picked up something that looked like a crossbow. He fit the bow with a strange-looking arrow. The tip had a spring-loaded clamp attached to it instead of an arrowhead. Tom tied a thin rope to the shaft. He took aim at the grate. The bow twanged. The arrow flew across the river, the rope unfurling behind it. The arrow clanged against the metal grate and fell into the water.

"Shoot!" whispered Tom. Izzy and Hen helped him reel in the rope. "It's too dark. I can barely see what I'm aiming for."

Fireflies began to flicker around them. Tom took another shot. This time, the clamp latched onto one of the bars like teeth.

"You did it!" said Hen.

Tom took the free end of the rope and fed it through another one of his machines: a jumble of pulleys with wooden handles on either side.

"This is the Zipper," he said. "I made it to get feedbags up to the barn loft without killing my back. With this, you girls won't have to do a thing. Just hold on tight to the handles, and it'll take you to the other side all by itself. Once you reach the grate, just send it back across. When it's my turn, I'll pull myself hand over hand. Izzy, I think you'd better go first. That way, you can catch your sister when she comes across."

Izzy slung the strap of her wool bag across her chest, then grabbed the handlebars of the Zipper and stepped into the river. She sucked in a breath when the frigid water spilled over the top of her boots.

Tom held the other end of the rope taut. He nodded to her. "Go on. Just pull that switch on the side."

Izzy waded farther in. When the water was up to her stomach, she flicked a metal switch on the Zipper. Something inside it clicked, and the machine whizzed along the rope, dragging her with it. Air bubbled out of her woolen clothes. They made her so buoyant, she floated almost entirely on the water's surface. When the Zipper reached the grate, Izzy grabbed the bars and wrapped her legs around them. The water flowed swiftly past the bars into the dark channel. Izzy's hand brushed against a heavy padlock submerged below the surface. She hoped Tom had brought something in his bag that could break it. Shivering, she reached up to the Zipper and flipped the switch to send it back to the shore.

Izzy watched nervously as Hen came across. But her

sister held tight, and a few minutes later, she had reached the grate too.

Just as Tom stepped into the water, they heard shouting from the bridge. Metal clanged, and the city doors swung open. Goblin boots pounded over the stone, followed by the unmistakable shrieks of the Unglers. Izzy made Hen duck down until only their heads bobbed above the water. The goblins held the Unglers on leashes like bloodhounds. Another dozen goblins on horseback thundered after them, riding out in the direction of the Edgewood.

As the last line of soldiers crossed the bridge, one of them shouted, "Look there! Someone on the riverbank!"

"Get down there and see what he's doin'!" shouted another goblin.

"Oh no!" Izzy whispered. "They spotted Tom!"

Tom dropped his end of the rope. He kicked his bag into the water and held both hands overhead. The two goblins rode down the riverbank and dismounted. One jabbed his finger into Tom's chest while the other searched his pockets. The river was too loud for Izzy to hear what they were saying. She held her breath and tried to stop her teeth from chattering. If the goblins looked across the water, she and Hen would be caught. The guards each grabbed one of Tom's arms and dragged him up the riverbank, over the bridge, and into the castle.

"Now what do we do?" whispered Hen.

Izzy reached down and jerked the padlock. "It's no good. It's locked."

Hen edged one shoulder between the bars of the grate. "I—I think I can make it…"

"Careful. Don't get stuck."

Hen's head scraped against the metal as she pushed through the bars. She turned with a huge smile on her face. "I did it! I'm—oh no!" Her fingers slipped off the grate.

"Hen, no!"

Izzy grasped for her hand, but the current had already pulled her out of reach. Hen's arms flailed and splashed as she sped away and disappeared into the channel.

FOUR AND TWENTY
BLACKBIRDS

Izzy THREW HERSELF AT the grate. She wedged her shoulder between the bars and pushed as hard as she could. It was no good. She was too big.

"Ugh, come on!"

Izzy had never wished she was smaller until now. She shut her eyes and willed herself to make it. "Come on, come *on!*" With one last brain-squishing push, she was through.

She took a big breath and let go of the bars. "Hen! I'm coming!"

Izzy swam with the current, calling her sister's name. Her voice echoed off the stone walls surrounding her. She couldn't see anything in the dark channel. She swallowed a gulp of water. As she coughed it up, she heard a small voice coming from downstream.

"Here!" gurgled Hen. "I'm over here!"

Izzy swam ahead, following the sound. She pawed at the water all around her until her fingers touched fabric.

"I've got you!"

She pulled Hen close and helped her turn onto her back. Luckily, Tom's wool clothes were the perfect flotation devices. They bobbed at the surface, catching their breath as the current swept them farther into the darkness. Hen's teeth were chattering loudly. They needed to get out of the water soon, or they'd both freeze.

"Keep kicking your legs to stay warm," said Izzy.

She did the same, and the toe of her boot hit something solid. The current slowed, and sloshing, mechanical noises filled the darkness. A few more yards and Izzy could reach the bottom with both feet. She bobbed along on her toes, swinging her arms to either side of them. Her fingers grazed slimy stone walls, then the walls disappeared, replaced with a stone ledge a few inches above the water.

"Come on, Hen. Over here!"

Izzy pulled her sister to the side and hauled her out of the water onto cold flagstones. She opened her eyes wide but couldn't see anything. The rhythmic mechanical sounds echoed loudly all around them.

"This must be the pump room," said Izzy. "I think we made it!"

Tom had dressed them in his thickest, oiliest wool. Even after swimming through the river, they were only partially soaked through. When Izzy opened her bag, she was shocked to find everything inside was dry. It was like magic—Tom's own special sort of magic. She worried about him. If they were going to help him—or anyone else—they needed to get up into the castle in a hurry.

Izzy heard a loud scritch. She looked up to see the bright light of a match glowing between Hen's fingers.

Hen grinned and scratched the side of her nose. "I borrowed some of Tom's matches. You know—just in case."

"Uh-huh," said Izzy skeptically. But this time, she was thankful for her sister's fascination with flames.

Once they were dressed in their own clothes, Hen lit another match, and they began to look for a way out. The water from the river swirled in a stone pool in the center of the room. Along the wall, bellows wheezed and wheels whirred, pumping the water out of the pool and into copper pipes that disappeared into the ceiling. They reminded Izzy of the design of Tom's house. Beside the machinery, they found a narrow wooden door. Izzy pushed it open. An unlit stairwell wound up and out of sight. Hen's match went out.

"We don't have many left," she whispered. "Should I light another one?"

"Save them. We can climb stairs in the dark."

She took Hen's hand, and they started to climb. Small, unseen creatures clicked and squeaked at their feet, scuttling out of their way. Izzy was in too much of a hurry to dwell on what they might be. She knew it must be way past midnight by now. They had climbed countless steps when they finally came to a landing and a wooden door with a thin beam of light shining beneath it.

"If we peeked out into the castle, do you think you'd be able to recognize where we are?" Izzy whispered.

"I think so."

Izzy swung the door inward the slightest crack. Hen put her face to it.

She turned back to Izzy, smiling excitedly. "Yes, I know where we are!" she whispered. "This is the first floor—"

"First floor! But we've been climbing forever!"

Hen pointed at the crack. "I know, but I'm telling you, this is the ground level. You go down that way, and you get to the castle gates that lead out to the rest of the city. Over that way, there's a little courtyard that—"

Izzy cupped her hand over Hen's mouth. She'd heard voices. She didn't dare shut the door in case someone noticed. The girls held stone still and listened. Boots stomped closer and stopped just outside the stairwell.

"All you do is complain," said a nasally voice. "Least you only have to guard one of 'em. It'll be easy."

Izzy put her eye to the crack. It was a trio of goblin guards. She recognized Blister's pimply nose. One of his comrades was so round, he was almost a perfect sphere. He wrung his fleshy hands and shifted on his feet.

"He may only be one, but he's wild," moaned the round

guard. "You saw Pustule's hand. That Bretabairn nearly bit clear through his thumb. I could see the bone!"

"There ain't anyone left to guard him," said Blister. "Everyone else was sent out with the Unglers. Morvanna says they told her there's one more Changeling in the Edgewood, and she won't let no one rest till it's found."

"Yeah," said the nasally one. "And the two of us got to get back over the mountain to look for them scrubby little girls."

Hen squirmed. Izzy squeezed her to be still.

"And there ain't a wyvern alive strong enough to carry you." Blister poked the fat one's belly and laughed. "So, like it or not, you're comin' to the garden."

The fat goblin whined as they continued walking past. Izzy waited until they had stomped out of earshot.

"Did you hear that?" she whispered. "The wild one they're talking about must be Selden. Hen, do you know where they're going?"

"It's the courtyard I was telling you about. Morvanna calls it a garden, but everything in it is dead."

"Hopefully that doesn't include Selden! You stay right here behind this door. I'm going to see if I can get close to him."

Izzy opened the door a little farther and edged out into the hallway. She tiptoed down the hall, hugging the walls until she reached an archway that opened to the outside. Izzy crouched behind one of the huge urns that decorated either side of the arch. She peered around the corner into the courtyard.

Smoking torches threw an oily light onto the stone walls. The castle rose high around the square enclosure. In the farthest corner, Selden lay underneath a heap of netting in his wolf form. His eyes were closed, and he breathed steadily. The net was cinched shut at the top with a silver cord. The end of the cord stretched to the wall, where it was tied to a thick metal spike. There was no sign of Dree or Lug anywhere.

A goblin with a long, sunken face sat in a wooden chair near Selden with a bowl in his lap. He cracked nuts between his teeth while blackbirds hopped from one foot to the other, waiting for him to drop one.

The long-faced goblin spat a nutshell onto the floor at the other goblins' feet. "It's my turn to go off duty, and I'm takin' it. I been watchin' that mangy thing for hours now." He jutted his chin at Selden.

The fat goblin hung back, watching Selden nervously. "I thought Her Majesty already took care of all the Bretabairn."

The long-face shook his head. "The Weaver can only do so many at a time. We're to guard this one till sunup. That's when the Weaver'll be ready to take him."

The other goblins seemed to shrink down and shudder whenever the long-face said the word "Weaver." Izzy wondered who he was talking about.

The fat goblin still hadn't taken a step closer. "Pustule said that boy bit him good…"

The long-face sneered. "Pustule got too close, that's all. That boy can Change all he wants, but he cain't get out 'less I let him. Watch."

He stood and drew a wooden club from his belt. He stalked up behind the sleeping wolf and whacked him on the spine with it. Selden sprung up and howled. He went crazy, snarling and clawing for the goblin. But the long-face stayed just out of reach, and the only thing Selden managed to do was to cinch the cord tighter around the stake in the wall.

The goblins cackled wickedly. The long-face handed his club to his fat replacement. "Here. He gives you any trouble, just give him a taste of this."

The long-face joined the other two goblins as they turned and marched back into the castle. Izzy squeezed herself between the wall and the urn and held her breath until they were gone. Back in the courtyard, the fat goblin had slid the chair backward a few feet. He cracked open one of the nuts and sucked out the insides.

"Blech!" he said, spitting it out again. He flung the rest of the bowl out on the ground. Wings fluttered as all the black-birds descended on the remains.

"I should've offered those nasty snacks to you," the goblin said to Selden. "You sure won't get any food where you're headed." He chuckled as he eased down farther into the chair and crossed his arms over his swollen belly. "No tricks now, or you know what I'll do." He patted the club at his side.

Selden stared at him. He growled but didn't lash out again. After a moment, he laid his head on his forepaws and shut his eyes. The fat goblin's chin dipped lower and lower until it rested on his chest. He began to snore.

Izzy got to her feet and tiptoed into the courtyard. Boxes of perfectly pruned trees had been placed along the perimeter, their leaves brittle and yellow. She crept behind the planter boxes while the goblin snored on his chair. If she was going to reach Selden, she would have to walk across the center of the courtyard, right by him.

The blackbirds pittered around the guard's feet, unheard over his snoring. Izzy took a deep breath and started across, keeping her eye on the iridescent birds. She wished she could be as featherlight as one of them, with tiny scaled feet tapping softly across the stone floor. The birds eyed Izzy, twitching their heads like little dragons, but they didn't fly away.

Selden jolted upright when Izzy touched his shoulder. The blackbirds spooked and took to the battlements high overhead. The goblin snorted in his sleep but didn't wake.

"Shhh!" whispered Izzy. "It's me!"

"What are you—"

Izzy put her finger to her lips. She pointed at the sleeping guard, then to the cord. She motioned for Selden to move closer to the metal stake. She needed some slack if she was going to untie it.

Selden quietly dragged himself closer to the wall. Izzy

hesitated before starting on the knot. She tried not to dwell on the idea of touching Morvanna's spittle as she set to work. She remembered from her experience with Lug's snare that the silver cord was impossible to break if put in tension. But it was actually quite slippery and easy enough to loosen if she worked with it gently. The goblins had been much clumsier at tying this knot than the Unglers had. It only took a few minutes to get it free.

Selden Changed back to himself as the net fell at his feet. Without a word, Izzy started to tiptoe back to the courtyard entrance with Selden following behind. A handful of black-birds returned to hunt for more dropped snacks. As she watched them hop around the empty net, she had an idea. She leaned over and whispered it to Selden.

He nodded and Changed into a stoat. He stalked behind one of the blackbirds and pounced on it. Once he had it pinned, he Changed back to himself. Cupping the bird gently in his hands, he crept back to the net and slipped it inside. Then he cinched up the net and tied the cord back on the stake.

Hen clapped with glee when she saw them come back down the hall. She let them into the stairwell and quietly shut the door.

Selden hugged both of them. "You two are the absolute last people I ever expected to see!"

"Are you OK?" asked Izzy.

"I'm fine except for this walloping headache," he said, rubbing the back of his head.

"Where are Lug and Dree?" asked Hen.

"I don't know," said Selden. "They separated us as soon as they brought us to the castle. Peter and the queen came down to check on us. I swear, Morvanna looked at me like she wanted to eat me alive. She wanted to cut out our hearts right away, but Peter said she should take us to the Weaver first. He said it would make our power last longer."

"Everyone keeps talking about this Weaver," said Izzy. "Who is it?"

"I have no idea," said Selden. "I've never heard of him. But Peter and Morvanna also called him something else. Lacquer, Lacrumb…"

"Lacrimo?" asked Hen.

"That's it!" said Selden. "How did you know?"

"Once, when Peter was showing me around the castle, he took me to this huge ballroom. There's a secret passage in one of the walls that leads to a tower. He told me there's a treasure there, but Morvanna has to keep it hidden, because the goblins won't guard it. They're too scared to get close to Lacrimo."

"Do you remember how to get to the secret passage?" asked Selden.

Hen hesitated. "The castle is confusing. But I remember the ballroom is at the very top. As high as you can go. But we didn't use these stairs. We used the main ones."

"Let's hope both stairways lead to the same place," said Izzy. "Come on. We have to hurry!"

They climbed the dark steps, two at a time at first, then slower as they got higher. It was almost as hard as hiking over Mount Mooring. Finally, they reached the last landing. Izzy cracked the door and listened. Silence. She held it open for Hen to poke her head out.

"Does this look familiar?" Izzy asked.

"I—I think so…" Hen stepped out of the doorway. Straight ahead was a pair of tall doors. Hen pushed one of them open and looked inside. She nodded at Izzy with her gap-toothed grin. "Yes! This is it!"

The ballroom was vast, big enough to swallow up Izzy's entire house. Floor-to-ceiling windows lined the walls on either side. It was so quiet that Izzy felt she could hear the dust whirring through the beams of moonlight. She and Selden followed Hen as quietly as their boots would allow. They walked between rows of thick pillars that stood spaced all throughout the room like a forest of stone trees.

Hen shimmied across the marble floor in her socks. "Don't you wish we had roller skates right now?" she whispered.

"I can think of a million other things to wish for," said Izzy. "Are you sure you know where you're going?"

"Definitely sure."

At the far end of the room, Hen counted the panels along the bottom of the wall. "…twelve…thirteen. This is the one!"

She knelt down and felt all around the molding. "Peter pushed it a certain way…like this…"

Click. The panel swung inward on a hidden hinge, revealing a black passageway.

"Hen, you're amazing!" said Selden.

Hen lit one of the last matches and held it into the passage. Selden and Izzy leaned in over her shoulder. A wooden spiral stair wound up and down, disappearing into darkness in both directions.

Hen pointed to the steps leading up. "Peter said that's where Lacrimo lives. At the very top. And those"—she pointed at the downward stair—"go down to another secret entrance in the stables. That's the only other way to get into the tower."

Izzy stood up and looked out the ballroom windows. The lowest stars were already starting to fade. "We have to hurry. It's almost dawn, and that's when the goblins said Morvanna was going to take Selden to the Weaver. Our blackbird trick isn't going to fool her for long."

Selden looked down into the passage and frowned. "Once we get Lug and Dree, we could escape out through the stables. But what if Morvanna comes while we're still on the stairs? We're dead if she catches us on those narrow steps."

"What if she couldn't get to them?" asked Hen.

"What do you mean?"

Hen grinned like she just found out where their parents hid the Christmas presents. She pulled a small bag out of her pocket and showed it to Izzy. Izzy could smell what it was before she even opened it.

"Blitzing powder! Did you take this from Tom's house too?"

Hen scratched her nose. "Sorry, I forgot to tell you earlier." She jumped up and ran to the nearest column. She rubbed her palm over the stone and double-checked the bag. "I think I've got enough. I can take out these three columns at the same time. That should totally block this entire wall."

"Are you *nuts*?"

"No, no, listen to her," said Selden.

Hen drew imaginary lines on the ground with her finger. "I can set it up so that we can light it, then make it out the secret passage before it blows. We can time it just right so it'll block Morvanna and give us enough time to escape out of the castle!"

Selden nodded. "It's a great idea. You get it all ready, and Izzy and I will go upstairs and get Lug and Dree."

"Ugh, fine," said Izzy. "But I'm taking these." She plucked the matchbox out of Hen's pocket and stuffed it into her own. "Knowing you, you'd get too excited and blow us all up."

Selden pulled Izzy by the sleeve. "Come on. Let's get moving!"

Izzy followed him reluctantly. As they crawled into the secret passageway, she got one more look at Hen. Her sister held the drawstring bag in her teeth while she made a little mound of powder on the floor.

"You do realize you just put our lives in the hands of a seven-year-old?" Izzy whispered to Selden.

He shushed her and started heading up. The steps were so steep they had to climb hand over hand, like a ladder. The air in the tower smelled old. Izzy tried not to touch the walls. She wondered if Selden felt it too—the fear that the very stones held some kind of secret. Izzy wasn't sure she wanted to know what it was.

When they finally reached the door at the top, they paused for a moment to catch their breath.

"Are you ready?" Selden whispered.

She nodded. Together, they leaned on the door and pushed it open.

The smell of decay and dust flew in their faces. As they stepped inside, they heard a hoarse voice. "All is ready, Your Maj—oh! How nice! Do come in, children. The Weaver welcomes you!"

THE MASTER WEAVER

SICKLY CANDLELIGHT THREW DARK shadows around the
room. In the corner, a very old man sat on a wooden stool
in front of a large spinning wheel. His shoulders were so
stooped that his back mounded up behind him like a tumor.
He motioned to them to come inside. Izzy clutched Selden's
sleeve. The man had six skeletal arms, with one long, bony
finger at the end of each one.

"At long last! Someone to admire my masterpiece!" croaked
the old man. "Come, come! Surely you are not frightened of
frail, old Lacrimo? I so seldom have visitors here, so seldom.
For months, I see no one but the flies." His beady eyes
skimmed the room as if searching for one.

"Who are you?" asked Selden, his voice echoing off the walls.

The old man's many joints clicked and popped as he stood
up from his stool and walked toward them. "Isn't that a pity?
There was a time when you would not have had to ask that

question. My name was once known by every fairy in this part of the world. But no more, no more. Poor old Lacrimo, kept in obscurity, his talents hidden away. But no matter. It is not the recognition I seek. I am satisfied that my life's work will live on after I am gone."

Lacrimo continued limping forward as he spoke. He was a head shorter than Selden, but his long arms had twice the span. "Have you not heard of me, children?" he asked pitifully. "The Master Weaver?"

Izzy clung to Selden as he took a step back. "No, we haven't heard of you," he said. "And we don't have time to talk about the past. We were told this is where the Changelings are kept. If that's not true, then we'll leave."

"You heard right, my boy! You heard right!" Lacrimo's eyes danced excitedly. "That is what I am trying to explain. They are here!"

Selden and Izzy looked around the bare room. "Where? Tell us!" demanded Selden.

The old man swept four of his arms to the wall beside them. "Here! Before your very eyes!"

The dark shadows had prevented them from noticing an enormous tapestry that covered the entire wall, stretching from floor to ceiling.

Lacrimo clattered back to his stool and retrieved a second candle to illuminate the tapestry. "Is it not grand? Is it not the finest piece of art you have ever laid eyes on?"

Izzy and Selden stepped closer to it. *Grand* was an understatement. The tapestry depicted a woodland scene of plants and animals. Over a dozen birds and beasts danced in a circle in the clearing between the expertly woven trees. The many-colored fibers were woven so tightly that it looked more like a painting than a piece of fabric. When the light flickered across the threads, the figures almost looked alive. But there was also something sinister about it. The looks on the animals' faces were of surprise or fear, as if they had been frightened and frozen in that position.

"This is the masterpiece of all my work," said Lacrimo. "It has been the most laborious by far. Just look at how I have captured their very breath within the threads. It looks as if they could leap out of the weaving, does it not?" He chuckled to himself. "But they cannot. No, they cannot."

Selden went from one animal to the next, looking at them closely. He spun around. "What did you do to them?"

Lacrimo paid no attention to him. He chattered on like a madman, staring at his beloved tapestry. "When she brought them to me, the pitiful little creatures, I doubted my abilities. Oh yes, even I did not believe I could execute such a request. But after years of work, I have fulfilled her wish. *Make the knots tight*, she said. *It must bind them for eternity.* As if I would do less!"

His face screwed up into a miserable pout. "Of course, she never told me she would come from time to time and snatch away their heart-threads. Oh, she says she only takes a few at a time, but it has marred the effect of my work." He clucked his tongue. "I suppose not everyone shares my artistic vision."

Izzy leaned closer to the tapestry. She noticed tiny frayed patches at some of the animals' chests where strands of thread had been pulled away. "Selden," she whispered, pulling him close so he could see. "One of the ingredients in Morvanna's elixir was a *thread*!"

Selden had found a section of the tapestry where the thread was a brighter color, like it had been freshly woven. A shaggy bear cowered with his hands over his head. A white butterfly clung to his shoulder.

Selden turned to Lacrimo. "Get them out of there. Unweave them, or whatever it is you do."

"Unweave them?" scoffed Lacrimo. "My powers are in creation, dear boy, not destruction. I cannot unmake my work once it is finished."

"Then you're a murderer," said Selden through clenched teeth.

Lacrimo put one finger to his heart. "Murder? No, this was not murder, but a sacrifice. For art."

In a ripple of black, Selden transformed into a snarling leopard. He turned to the tapestry and, with one swipe of his claws, drew a gash through one of the trees.

Lacrimo's shriek rang off the stone walls.

Selden rent another deep cut into the corner of the tapestry.

"No! Get away from it, you monster!" Lacrimo ran to his

stool. He looped two bony fingers around a pair of silver shears. Holding them out, he ran straight at Selden.

"Watch out!" shouted Izzy.

The leopard ducked aside at the last moment. Lacrimo lost his balance and fell toward the tapestry. The scissors ripped another hole. He flung them away from him and clung to the folds of fabric for support.

"Oh, my masterpiece!" he sobbed. He clutched at the ruined tapestry, wrapping himself in it like a robe.

Izzy heard a creaking sound and looked up. With each tug, the heavy brass rod that supported the fabric bowed outward on its brackets. Selden knelt at the foot of the weaving, back to his boy form, staring at the madman in disgust.

"Selden! Hurry, get away from there!" Izzy rushed over to him, pulled him up to his feet, and dragged him to the far side of the room.

With a crunching crack, the brass rod tore free from its brackets, pulling out huge pieces of stone from the wall. Lacrimo screamed as the folds of his tapestry fell on top of him. The rod and chunks of stone landed on him with a heavy thud.

Selden and Izzy huddled on the floor until the rock dust settled from the air. The tapestry lay in a rumpled, massive heap. There was no movement or sound from its folds.

"Oh my gosh," whispered Izzy. "Do you think he's—"

Selden drew himself up to stand. "Come on. Help me."

Together, they lifted each end of the heavy brass rod and

dragged it to the other side of the room. The tapestry spread out along the floor, covering it nearly from wall to wall. At the foot of the weaving lay a small, crumpled heap.

"I can't look," said Izzy, covering her eyes.

Selden went over to the heap and knelt down. "He's dead," he said flatly. He stood up and stepped lightly on top of the masterpiece. He walked to the center, where the animals danced in their ring, sat down, and put his head in his hands. "Now no one will ever get them out."

Izzy walked over to him and put her hand on his shoulder, not knowing what to say. The tapestry was dusty, with three huge gashes near the bottom border where Selden and the scissors had slashed it. Even from the underside, it was still breathtaking. When the light flickered, it almost looked as if the fur on the animals shivered a bit.

Izzy's forehead broke out into beads of sweat in the close, musty room. She shrugged off her jacket and let it fall beside her. As it fell, something tiny and blue rolled out of the inside pocket and onto the fabric. Izzy hurriedly bent down to pick up Marian's little bottle. She'd forgotten all about it. The bottle's stopper had come loose. Before she could replace it, one drop of bloodred liquid seeped out onto a woven rosebud. Izzy bent closer and watched as the liquid soaked into the fibers. She could hear a faint hissing sound. She jumped back as the threads surrounding the bud unraveled and it blossomed into a real rose whose fragrance began to fill the dank room.

"No way," Izzy whispered.

She turned the bottle over and read the label. *Root Revive.* What had Marian said it was for? *Dead trees.* Izzy remembered all the books about magic she had seen on the coffee table in the old woman's house. Maybe there was more to the little bottle than just a country garden remedy. Izzy bent down and plucked the rose free from the tapestry.

"Selden, you have to see this!"

He looked up. His eyes grew wide when he saw the rose in her hand. "Do you think—"

Izzy didn't wait for him to finish. She ran to kneel beside the bear and butterfly. She placed two drops of the liquid on both of their heads. She stood up and stepped back as the drops soaked in. The tapestry heaved upward with a ripping sound, and they both popped out of the fibers onto their feet. Dree and Lug nearly fell over as they Changed back into themselves.

Izzy grabbed Dree's elbow to prop her up. Dree blinked over and over, adjusting her eyes to the light. Finally, she focused on the face in front of her. "Wh-what are you doing here?"

Izzy laughed and hugged her tight.

Selden had his arms around Lug, who sat on the floor. "Terrible, so terrible," said Lug with a shiver. "Morvanna— she wrapped us up in—in spiderwebs!"

Selden blew warm air onto his friend's hands. He looked up at Izzy. "What about the rest of them? Do you think it will work?"

Izzy started with the figure of a little red squirrel with

a frayed patch on his white chest. She set two drops from Marian's bottle onto him and held her breath. The fibers hissed, and the squirrel sprung up to stand. With a shake of his head, he transformed into a young boy with a shock of auburn hair.

Selden approached him slowly, like he might turn to dust and vanish. "Olligan?" he whispered.

The boy reached out his hands. "Selden? Is that really you?" he said weakly.

Selden threw both arms around the boy's shoulders. "Yes, it's me!" He stepped backward and held Olligan at arms' length, looking him up and down. "Are you all right, Olli?"

"I—I think so. But I feel like I can't quite catch my breath." He rubbed his hand over his chest and shut his eyes. After a moment, they sprang open again. "Oh my goodness! Where are all the others?"

Izzy was already quick at work. She did the same to a golden antelope, a turtledove, then a greyhound. As each animal emerged from the tapestry and Changed into their child form, Lug and Dree rushed to them, calling out their names.

"Hiron! Chervil! Hale!"

Soon, fourteen boys and girls stood on the folds of the ruined masterpiece. They ranged in age from younger than Hen to a little older than Selden. They all shared the same bewildered expression. The Changelings with frayed heart-threads were weaker than the others. Their friends supported them until they could catch their breath and stand on their own. Izzy could tell from the tapestry that Morvanna had taken the heart-threads sparingly. She didn't want to think about what might have happened if the queen's harvesting had gone on much longer.

Dree had tears in her eyes, and Lug was hopping from one foot to the other in a joyful dance. Selden stood apart from everyone, watching. That cloud that had hung over him for so long was finally gone, replaced with an enormous smile.

Lug suddenly turned and picked Selden up in one arm and Izzy in the other. "You did it! You did it! Three cheers for Selden and Izzy!"

The other Changelings let out a whoop. They crowded around Selden and alternated between hugging him and jabbing him in the ribs. He laughed as they knocked him around. Izzy laughed too but stopped when she looked up at the tower window. All the stars were gone, and the sky glowed light gray.

"Selden, it's morning! We have to get back to Hen!"

Selden nodded. "Come on, everyone. Down the stairs and don't stop until you reach the stables at the very bottom!" He held the door open for all the Changelings as they filed out of Lacrimo's room.

Izzy followed behind, trying not to rush them. They were moving so slowly, still weak from their time spent in the tapestry. When they reached the secret panel that led to the ballroom, Selden turned to her.

"Do you want me to wait with you until the powder's lit?" he whispered.

"No, you need to go with the others," said Izzy. "I think they're all still a little dazed. We'll light the powder, then Hen and I will be right behind you."

Izzy nudged open the panel with her boot. She ducked down and crawled into the ballroom. The panel swung shut behind her. "Hen!" she said as she stood up. "It's time. Let's—"

The words died in her throat.

Hen stood in the center of the room. Good Peter stood behind her, both hands firmly on her shoulders.

Izzy started to run at him. "No, get away from her!"

A hand grabbed the back of her head and twisted its fingers into her hair.

"Not so fast, *sullen girl.*"

AN OLD FAMILIAR FACE

MORVANNA COILED THE HAIR around her fingers until Izzy felt like her scalp would rip away. She twisted Izzy's face up. The queen looked haggard, like she hadn't slept in days. Strands of white hair framed her lined face, and dark circles cradled her eyes.

"I just sent my wyverns over the mountain to fetch you," said Morvanna. "But here you are. It was quite the happy surprise to open the ballroom doors and find sweet Henrietta standing there."

Hen was on the verge of tears. "I'm sorry, Izzy! I didn't hear them coming!"

Peter squeezed her shoulders and made a shushing sound.

"I see you found Lacrimo's secret hiding place," continued Morvanna. Her voice was like a spider crawling into Izzy's ear. "Isn't he a marvel? It was Peter who found him and brought him to me. By now, the Weaver has finished adding my two most recent acquisitions to the tapestry. And this dirty ruffian is on his way to join them. It's just in time too. I'm all out of my elixir."

On the floor at the queen's feet, the blackbird squawked and fluttered beneath the silver net. Their trick had worked. But the real Selden wouldn't be safe for long. He and the others probably weren't even halfway down the stairs yet. Morvanna might even hear them once she climbed inside the passageway.

"Izzy, I did everything I was supposed to do," said Hen with a little sob.

"Quiet!" barked Morvanna. "Peter, take Henrietta back to my room. This mousy sister of hers is no use to me. I'll deal with her as soon as I take the boy upstairs."

Peter started to lead Hen toward the ballroom doors. "Izzy!" she shouted. "I did everything I said I'd do. *Everything.*" She raised both eyebrows and looked down at the floor.

Izzy followed her gaze. A thin line of black dust ran between the marble columns. A small pile of blitzing powder lay at the base of each one. Hen had done her job well. If they lit the powder now, it would bring half the ceiling down. The Changelings could get away. But Izzy and Hen would be trapped inside.

Morvanna picked up the net with her free hand and started dragging Izzy by the hair toward the hidden passage. Izzy locked eyes with her sister. Hen held up one thumb and wiggled it. Instantly, Izzy remembered Morvanna's nasty, nervous habit.

She reached up and found the corner of the queen's thumb. Izzy ripped into the tender, raw skin with her fingernails. Morvanna howled. She dropped Izzy and clutched her bleeding thumb to her stomach.

Hen wriggled out of Peter's grip. Izzy dug the matchbox out of her pocket and lobbed it to her sister. Hen caught it. She dropped to her knees. With one stroke, the match was lit, and a spark fizzed down the powder trail.

Izzy ran for Hen. "Get down, get down!"

Boom!

The blast knocked Izzy off her feet and slammed her onto the floor. She curled into a ball as chunks of marble rained down around her. The floor was still reverberating when she felt someone's hands on her shoulders. They pulled her up to her knees. Izzy saw a glimpse of fine velvet and knew it must be Good Peter, but it was hard to see anything else. Something wet and sticky was running into her eyes. She put her fingers to her forehead and held them out again. They came away red with blood.

Izzy pushed Peter off her. She held one hand to her forehead and looked around, trying to get her bearings. The blast had thrown her into the center of the ballroom. Stone dust swirled in the morning light that streamed through the shattered windows. The explosion had pulverized the columns and brought a huge section of the ceiling down with them. A mountain of rubble covered the entrance to the secret passage.

A few yards away, Izzy spotted a tangle of golden curls.

"Hen!" Izzy crawled to her sister and pushed the hair off her face. Hen's eyes were shut, and she looked so pale. "Oh, no, no, no..."

Peter knelt beside Hen and placed two fingers on the side of her neck. Izzy started to push him away but then realized what he was doing.

He waited a moment, counting her pulse, then looked up at Izzy. "She'll be all right."

"Oh, thank goodness!"

Peter gently scooped Hen up in his arms. Izzy followed him as he carried her to the corner of the room. He set her down behind one of the intact pillars.

Izzy held Hen's hands in hers. "It's going to be OK, clucky Hen," she whispered.

Hen moaned softly but didn't wake. Izzy heard a rustling sound coming from the wall of rubble. She leaned out past the edge of the column to see.

Near the rubble pile, the blackbird cawed and struggled in its net. Beside it, a mass of silk fabric stirred, and the queen staggered to her feet. She sucked the blood off her thumb and began to pace in front of the mound of broken stone.

Morvanna stretched her fingertips to the floor. She hummed a low song, like something chanted deep in a cat-acomb. The swirls in the marble tiles began to glow bright blue. She increased the tempo, and the swirls flickered and rose up from the floor. They grew and grew until they became cobras with curling hoods. The blue snakes swayed obediently beneath the queen's raised arms. One by one, she sent them headfirst into the rubble. When the cobras slammed into it, they shattered the stone and themselves into thousands of pieces. Izzy ducked back behind the pillar to shield herself from the flying debris. When she looked again, her spirits sank. The secret panel was clear.

Morvanna bent over, wheezing. Using her powers had aged her. White streaks ran through her hair, and her lips were thin and drawn.

She picked up the net, glaring at the bird inside. "No more delays." She swung open the panel.

A flash of inky fur sprang out.

Izzy gasped. "Selden!"

Morvanna dodged the black leopard just in time. Selden's paws skidded on the dusty floor as he whirled around to face her. He reared back to charge again. The queen raised another cobra from the floor and flung it at him, but he ducked, and it blasted into the wall behind him.

The queen and the leopard circled each other, eyes locked. Izzy watched them anxiously, her fists clenched tight to her chest.

Beside her, Peter patted his hands along the floor. "Where is it?" he whispered. "Please, you must help me find it!"

"Find what?" asked Izzy.

"My flute! I lost it in the blast. I must find it again!"

They heard the crash of stone and a yowl of pain. Izzy and Peter both leaned beyond the column to look. Selden had been hit. He limped backward, holding one paw off the ground.

Morvanna's hair was now completely white. Wrinkles covered her face and hands, and her throat sagged with age. But still she stood tall, like a grizzled warrior. More than ever, Izzy was convinced she had seen her before.

"I...should have known." Selden panted as he backed away. "You're just a...tired old...witch."

A witch? Izzy remembered what Marian had told her: *Only humans are witches.*

Of course. The queen had changed so much that Izzy hadn't noticed her ears. They were no longer pointed but perfectly, humanly round. And now Izzy realized why the queen looked so familiar. Before, Morvanna's youth and all her royal finery had prevented her from seeing it. Now the only thing missing were the farmer's clothes.

The old witch looked exactly like Marian.

The queen cackled harshly as she circled Selden. "Clever boy. Yes, that's right, I'm a witch. And I am old, but not tired, not yet. I've got more than enough power left to finish you off."

Selden paced in front of her, growling low. "That power isn't yours. Your magic is nothing but trickery."

"Ha! You fairies are all the same. You think you deserve your powers just because you were born with them. You bring us to your world and surround us with magic we're not allowed to have. You think we should be content to keep the balance of things—grow old and worn out doing honest, *human* work."

Morvanna reached behind her back and pulled a metal object from her waistband. Izzy strained to see what it was, but the witch held it down at her side, concealed in the folds of her skirt.

"I did work," she continued. "I worked myself to the bone. It took me decades of study to master my craft. By the time I did, I was an old woman. But then I learned I could change all that. I could be young again, strong again." A smile stretched across her bony face. "Your friends have bought me plenty of time to enjoy the fruits of all my hard work. My only regret is that I listened to Peter instead of cutting their hearts out from the very beginning. But there's still plenty of time for that." She pointed at Selden's chest. "I think I'll start with you."

Selden reared on his haunches and sprang at Morvanna with his claws out. She spun out of the way and slashed his hip with the dagger she held at her side. With a howl, he retreated backward.

"There it is!" Peter whispered to Izzy. "My flute! There, near Selden's feet. You have to help me. Create a diversion— draw Morvanna's attention away while I go get the flute."

"Who cares about your stupid flute?" said Izzy, choking on tears. "Can't you see that Selden's going to die? I hope your flute smashes into a million pieces. You deserve it for helping that witch!"

Peter grabbed her by the arms and spun her around to face him. "Look at me, you foolish girl! Can't you see that *helping* that witch was the only way I could protect the Changelings? I had to keep her close! I'm forbidden to harm her with my powers, but if I can get my flute, I may be able to do something to save Selden. Now you must get out there. I need your help!"

Izzy could barely make out the blur of Peter's face through her tears. "Why do you keep telling *me* to help him? I can't do anything!"

Peter peered deep into her eyes. "You really don't know, do you?"

"Know what?"

"Izzy…you're a Changeling."

CHANGELING HEART

THE REST OF THE world blurred, leaving Peter's face the only thing in focus. He whispered quickly, urgently.

"Eleven years ago, a friend gave me an orphaned fairy and asked me to hide it away. When I saw the infant, I immediately knew she was a Changeling. I took her to Earth. At the first house I came to, the family had just had a baby, born in the middle of the night, too early."

Izzy shook her head. "No...this is a lie."

"The family was sleeping," Peter continued. "They didn't realize their baby hadn't survived the night. I looked down at the Changeling in my arms. You looked so much like the other child. So I used my flute to round your ears, and then I switched you. I meant to come back for you later, but when I returned, you were gone. I left and forgot about you and about that house. When I stole Hen from the woods in Everton, I never dreamed she was your sister. If I had known, I never would have taken her. But what's done is done, and now you're here, and I need your help!"

Out on the ballroom floor, Izzy could hear Morvanna flinging more stone and Selden crying out wearily. Her shoulders heaved with sobs. "You're lying! This isn't true!"

"It is true! And you know it; I can see it in your eyes." Peter gave her a shake like he was trying to wake her from a nightmare. "Surely at some point in your life, you've realized your Changeling powers. Has there never been a time when you were all alone, when you Changed into something else? Think carefully!"

Izzy looked into Peter's black eyes. Her chest tightened, like all the air in the room was gone, but she couldn't make herself look away. And there, in those black, bottomless pools, she saw the image of a little red fox stalking up on her unsuspecting sister in a game of hide-and-seek. She saw it for only a moment, a fraction of a second, but that was enough.

Izzy's breath came back in one great gush as the realization hit her. The fox in the woods. The mouse in the sack of chestnuts. Even the blackbird in the courtyard only moments ago. She had told herself she was just pretending, that they were just her imagination. But now she knew the truth.

They were all her.

Peter released his grip on her arms. "There. I knew you'd come to your senses. Now will you *please* do something?"

Izzy had stopped crying, but her whole body still shook. "But—what do I do?"

"Something, anything!" whispered Peter, glancing worriedly around the edge of the pillar. "Whatever you have the ability to Change into. It doesn't have to be impressive, just confront Morvanna long enough for me to get my flute. Now that her powers are depleted, I may be able to subdue her."

Izzy just stared at him. Did he realize what he was asking her to do? "I can't Change. I don't know how!"

Peter hauled her up by the arm onto her feet. "If you've done it before, you can do it now. Hurry!"

He pushed Izzy to the wall on the east side of the room. Morning sunlight poured in through the broken windows, creating wide bands of light and darkness across the floor. Trembling head to foot, she hugged the wall. She circled closer to Selden and Morvanna, ducking beneath each window she passed so she could stay in the shadows.

Izzy slipped off her boots and tiptoed carefully over the shattered glass and marble. Peter told her to cause a distraction, but what should she Change into? She knew she could be a fox, a mouse, and a blackbird. Was there anything else? Something that could fight the old witch?

In the center of the room, Morvanna stood with her back to Izzy, her hair a tangled nest of white. She jabbed her dagger at Selden. He lunged aside, but Morvanna feinted and switched hands. She sunk the blade deep into his shoulder. He screamed and thrashed away from her. As he kicked across the floor, he Changed back into his boy form.

Izzy left the shadows and crept toward Morvanna. The wound on her head throbbed, and her heart thundered in her chest. She gave up on Changing into anything ferocious. At this point, she just needed to Change into *something*. A fox. She had done it before—surely she could do it again.

A fox, just a simple, little fox, thought Izzy. A few yards from the witch, she remembered Lug's words: *It comes naturally. Just like breathing.*

Morvanna stepped toward Selden with the tip of her blade pointed right at his heart.

Izzy took a breath and shouted, "*Stop!*"

The witch spun around. When she saw Izzy, a black-toothed smile spread across her face. She started to cackle. Izzy looked down at herself in dismay. She was no different. She hadn't managed to Change into anything at all.

"The sullen girl just can't seem to stay away!" said Morvanna. "Don't worry, dear. I haven't forgotten about you."

Izzy trembled, looking up at the witch. Even old and withered, Morvanna towered over her.

The queen adjusted her grip on the dagger. "Maybe you've come to beg me for mercy. But why should I give it to you? Life has certainly never given it to me."

Izzy glanced at Selden, curled in pain on the floor. Beneath him, the growing pool of blood reflected his body like a dark mirror.

A mirror.

Izzy filled her lungs with air and let go.

The witch raised her dagger high above her head. "I think it's time you learned just how unmerciful this world can be." Morvanna looked up at the barbed point. She started to drive it straight down at Izzy.

The witch gasped. Her blade clattered to the floor.

She stood facing not a mousy little girl but a perfect, youthful version of her own self. The old queen gaped at her double. She touched her own sunken cheek, and the girl facing her did the same, but her skin was as smooth and white as cream.

Izzy stood straight-backed and tall, just like the queen she had first seen at the Apple Festival. With all her focus, she imagined she *was* that fairy queen, imperious and proud. She took another breath, relishing the strength rippling through her muscles. The real Morvanna straggled forward, her open mouth exposing rotten teeth.

"Yes, this is what I was meant to be; this is what I worked so hard for," Morvanna whispered, mesmerized with her young Likeness.

Izzy took a step back, holding the witch's gaze.

All the ferocity had drained out of Morvanna, replaced with a bone-weariness. She looked down at her wrinkled hand, then back up at her reflection's young face. "I lost so much time, so many years... They slipped through my fingers like smoke..."

The sadness in Morvanna's voice broke Izzy's concentration. Beneath the young queen's cold disdain, she felt her own emotions welling up. She tried to tamp them back down, but she couldn't help it. She felt sorry for the old witch.

The Likeness wavered. Izzy could feel it like a slight shiver running down her back. Pity was not something the young Morvanna would have felt, not even for her future self. She squared her shoulders and stilled her breath, trying to focus. Izzy knew she had to hold on to her form just a little while longer. Out of the corner of her eye, she could see Good Peter creeping across the ballroom toward Selden, where the silver flute lay on the floor near his feet.

Izzy stepped slowly backward, luring Morvanna along with her, away from Selden and Peter. She backed up until her satin shoes crunched over broken glass and the backs of her knees touched the window ledge behind her. The sunlight streaming in through the open window fell harshly on Morvanna's face. The old witch leaned so close that Izzy could smell the stench of decay on her breath.

Peter reached for the flute, but it slipped from his fingers and pinged onto the floor.

The sound snapped the witch out of her daydream. She looked Izzy up and down, her eyes burning with wild hatred. *"How dare you!"*

Morvanna raised her hands and lunged at her Likeness's ivory neck. In an instant, Izzy let the form slip off her like a silk robe. Plain brown hair replaced the fiery red, and all her regal splendor vanished. The cut on her forehead ached as she shrunk down to her normal self. But she was small again, and small was just what she needed to be.

Quick as a fox, she ducked down below the window ledge. Above her, the witch clawed at her vanishing reflection. Terror spread over Morvanna's face as she realized her mistake. She pinwheeled her arms to stop herself from plummeting out the open window, but it was too late. As she tumbled over the ledge, she twisted like a cat. At the last minute, she grasped Izzy's collar, yanking her headfirst out the window behind her.

Izzy felt a rush of air as she started to fall. Then rough hands grabbed her ankles, and her body jerked to a stop. The collar of her jacket ripped away in the witch's fingers.

Morvanna continued falling, down, down, past the high, sheer walls of her castle.

Izzy swayed by her feet, all the blood rushing to her head. The sky and the ground seemed to switch places. She shut her eyes.

Above her, she heard a dog barking. A gruff voice said, "Hold on, child, I've got you!"

Izzy opened her eyes and looked down. The witch's body lay on the stones far below, twisted all wrong.

Izzy shut her eyes and didn't dare open them again.

TIPPED UPSIDE DOWN

IZZY'S TONGUE WAS SO dry, she was positive someone had replaced it with a sock. She smacked her lips and slowly opened her eyes. A figure sat beside her bed. The window's bright light framed her white hair like a halo. When her face first started to come into focus, Izzy shrank back into the pillows. But then the woman smiled kindly, and the fear melted away.

"M-Marian?" Izzy croaked.

The old woman helped her sit up a little more. "That's right, child. But take it easy, take it slow."

"Where's Hen? Is she OK?"

"Yes, she's perfectly fine," said Marian, handing Izzy a glass of water. "Back to her fiery little self."

"And Selden? And all the others?"

"Selden's pretty battered, but he's a tough one. He's already on his feet again. And all the other Changelings are fine too, aside from worrying about you. Everyone wants to see you, but I told them you needed more time to rest."

Izzy relaxed a little and took a sip of water. She glanced up at the white stone walls of her room. "Are we still in the castle?"

"Yes. You've been sleeping on and off for almost two days. From what your friends told me, you haven't been taking very good care of yourselves. Sleeping too little and on the move too much. It's enough to make anyone exhausted."

"I can't believe you're really here," said Izzy. "After those cobwebs at Netherbee Hall, I thought I'd never see you again."

The old woman winked. "Marian Malloy getting beat by a bunch of dusty cobwebs? Nonsense."

Izzy sat up more. "But what happened? How did you get away?"

Something scritch-scratched at the door. Marian stood up to answer it. "I think it's best if I let someone else help me tell that story," she said, her hand on the doorknob. "Out of everyone who's wanted to see you, I think he's the most eager."

Marian opened the door, and a bundle of black fur and drool galloped to the bed.

"Dublin!" cried Izzy.

Dublin stood up on his hind legs and leaned onto the bed, sniffing and licking Izzy's face and hands. He would have leapt right into her lap if Marian hadn't held him down.

"What in the world are you doing here, Dub?"

"He showed up at Netherbee just after you left," said Marian. "Those webs had wrapped themselves so tight around me, I could barely wriggle my fingers. But your dog's a good listener. I told him to find the bag of herbs I brought and dump it out on the floor."

Izzy rubbed him behind his ears. "And he did it? Good boy, Dub!"

"I needed something that could get rid of those webs," said Marian. "I remembered a spell from one of my oldest books called, *Salt into Sparrows*. I didn't have any salt, but I did have mustard seed. Plenty of it. By the time those sparrows were finished, Netherbee Hall was licked clean. I guess the mustard made them feisty."

"And your *Root Revive* saved all the Changelings. Marian, you can do magic!"

"I tried for years to learn spells but couldn't ever get them to work for anything but the garden." Marian chuckled. "Maybe those gossips in Everton were right, and I do have a little witch in me after all."

The word *witch* made Izzy shiver. "Do you know about Morvanna?" she asked. "I mean, do you know what she looked like?"

Marian nodded grimly. "Once everything was over, Good Peter let me take a look at her. There's no mistake. I'm the Changeling who took her place all those years ago."

Izzy was struck by how the two women were alike and

different at the same time. They had the same face, but Marian looked radiant compared to the old witch. Decades of laughter and sun had given Marian her wrinkles, while Morvanna's face had been ravaged by years of jealousy and spite.

"Marian, I thought I saw you in the crowd at the Apple Festival. Was that you?"

"Yes, we must have just missed each other. After I got out of the Edgewood, I came here to Avhalon to look for you."

"You're lucky the Unglers didn't find you. Morvanna would have cut out your heart."

Marian nodded. "I guess we're both lucky in that regard."

Then Izzy remembered everything—Good Peter's story, the way it felt to take on Morvanna's Likeness, and the strange sensation of letting it go again.

Izzy leaned back into the pillows. "So it's really true," she said. "I'm a Changeling."

Marian placed her hand over Izzy's. "All those years, your grandmother and I worked to keep the Piper from taking you. We had no idea he already had."

Izzy closed her eyes and shook her head. "All this time, I've thought of myself as one thing, and now it turns out I'm not that person. I'm not even a *person* at all. Back home, I never felt like I fit in. Now I understand why."

It was all so confusing. Everything Izzy thought she knew about herself was wrong. Her parents weren't really her parents. "Izzy" wasn't even her real name. She held her sore forehead, feeling very much like a snow globe that had been tipped upside down.

Marian put a papery hand to Izzy's cheek. "My dear girl, child or Changeling, you have a whole mess of loved ones who care for you. In fact, there's a couple of them waiting in the next room who will be real mad at me if I don't let you go and see them. Do you feel up to it?"

"I don't know…"

"Well, up to it or not, you're going. It won't do you any good to sit here and mope."

Marian helped Izzy get out of bed and get dressed. Her shirt and trousers were clean and mended. Dublin sniffed curiously at her newly polished boots. She stood in front of a tall mirror and brushed out her hair, careful to avoid the tender cut at her hairline. As she brushed her hair away from her ears, she let out a little cry. They were as pointed as Marian's. If she had any lingering doubts about being a Changeling, there was the proof, staring her right in the face.

"I don't know if I can get used to this," she said, brushing her hair forward again.

Marian took the brush and used it to push her toward the door.

Izzy and Dublin walked into an ornate parlor where Dree and Lug sat across from each other at a round table, playing a game on a checkerboard with pieces shaped like owls.

Dree plunked one of her pieces next to Lug's and shouted,

"*Prenso!* That's three in a row for me!" She turned and saw Izzy standing at the door. "Finally. What took you so long to get out of bed? You been fighting witches or something?"

Lug's chair clattered to the floor as he jumped up and scooped Izzy into his arms. "We have hardly left this room, waiting for you to wake up!"

"Easy, there," said Dree, standing up from her chair. She wore a new lavender dress with a lace hem. "Let's not crush her ribs before she's fully recovered."

Lug set Izzy back down. She wrapped her arms around his belly, breathing in his wet dog smell. Dublin jumped up and set his forepaws on Lug's chest, licking his cheeks.

"Ho, ho, there, friend!" said Lug, scratching his ears. "Izzy, your dog is just delightful. Do you know that when I first met him, I chattered on with him for a full fifteen minutes before I realized he wasn't one of the other Changelings?"

"He's pretty great," said Izzy, patting Dublin's back.

"Keeping pets was one of those human habits I never did understand." Lug gasped and put his fingers over his mouth. "Oh my goodness, I completely forgot! I got so used to thinking of you as a human that it's hard to remember you're not."

Izzy sighed. "It's hard for me to remember too."

"We heard all about the Likeness you did of Morvanna," said Dree. "How'd you come up with something like that on the spot?"

"The oldest Changeling trick there is," said a voice behind them. "Isn't that right, Izzy?"

They turned to see Selden standing in the doorway. He leaned on a crutch with one arm and held the other in a sling.

Izzy walked up to him and surveyed the cuts and scratches on his face. After what she'd seen him go through, it was amazing he was even alive. "Gosh, you look terrible. Are you feeling OK?"

"Me? Oh, sure. I love being bandaged up. Couldn't you tell?" Selden beamed, and Izzy suspected he really did like having some wounds to show off. He shook his head at her, his brown eyes wide. "I still can't believe you're one of *us*! And this whole time, none of us picked up on it. I guess spending so much time with humans really ruined you."

Izzy laughed. Now she knew Selden really did feel all right.

"That must be why the Unglers chased you when they found us in the Edgewood," said Dree. "We thought they were smelling us, but they were really smelling *you*."

"Oh, let's never talk about those nasty things again," said Lug with a shudder. "They've run back to the Norlorn Mountains with all the goblins, and good riddance!" He squeezed Izzy's shoulder. "Instead, let's talk about how talented our girl is! Not many Changelings could make a witch go thunderstruck at her own Likeness."

"I don't think I'm talented at all," said Izzy. "I tried to Change into so many different things, and I couldn't do it. In the end, I think I just got lucky."

"You just need more practice," said Dree. "You'll get better with time, especially with all of us to help you."

"It's going to be fantastic!" said Lug. "There's enough room in this castle for each of us to have our own room. You can have the one next to mine. It's got a bed, but never mind that. I'll build you a twig pallet, just like that one you loved back at Yawning Top."

The door creaked open, and a shock of auburn hair emerged from behind it. Olligan grinned at them toothily, then called over his shoulder. "Come on in—she's awake!"

The fourteen other Changelings skipped and bounded noisily into the parlor. Izzy cried out happily when Tom Diffley came in after them. One by one, they grabbed Izzy's hands and gave her hugs while Dublin danced in happy circles at their feet. Then they all started talking at once:

"I knew my Izzy would come up with something clever."

"A Changeling who didn't even know it? I've never heard of that before!"

"That puts our number at eighteen. I think that's lucky, don't you?"

"Is that more than a dozen?"

Each Changeling's eager face was fixed on hers, asking a hundred questions and offering advice. She couldn't get a word in.

Finally, she shouted, "I'll do anything you want. Just don't make me be a goblin or a fat lady!"

They all burst into laughter. Izzy felt a wonderful warmth,

like the sun was shining directly on her cheeks. So this was what it was like to be surrounded with friends. It had never happened to her before, but already she was hooked.

"Isn't this lovely?" chortled Lug. "Everyone together, just like it should be. All we need is little Hen, and we'd be a complete party."

Izzy stopped laughing. She'd forgotten all about Hen. "Does anyone know where she is?"

The Changelings murmured to one another, and someone said they'd seen her standing out in the hallway by one of the windows.

Izzy pulled herself away from the group and hurried to the door. "Sorry, I'll be right back," she called over her shoulder. "I just need to talk to my—to Hen—for a minute."

Her palms sweated as she walked out into the hall. If all the others knew she was a Changeling, then Hen must have heard about it too. How would Hen take the news that the person she thought was her sister really wasn't?

She found Hen sitting in a sunny window seat. Outside the window, the Avhal Mountains looked painted onto the sky, just like an illustration from one of Izzy's storybooks.

Hen heard her coming and stood up. She smiled, but it was the forced smile she wore for school pictures. "Hey, Marian told me you were up. Are you feeling better?"

"Yeah, a lot better. How about you—are you OK?" Izzy put her hand out to touch her sister's hand, then drew it back down. Hen looked stiff, like maybe she didn't want to be touched at all.

"Yeah, I woke up right after—you know, after what happened."

"So do you know about everything? About me, I mean."

Hen gazed back out the window and said softly, "There was this one time at our old house when we were playing hide-and-seek, and I thought I saw you turn into a fox for just a second. I told myself it was just my imagination, but I guess it really wasn't."

Even though she stood right there, Hen seemed miles away. Izzy wished she would bounce around, or give her that missing-teeth smile, or even get mad and yell at her. Anything would be better than not knowing what she was thinking.

"Hen, I know all this must be really weird and confusing. I'm confused too."

Hen tried to force another smile, but it quickly faded. She looked down at her feet. "I heard the Changelings talking about how they're going to teach you all this great stuff... And you'll have a new room... You won't have to share..." Her words broke into sobs.

Izzy held her arms out, and her sister fell into them.

Hen's little body heaved up and down as she stammered, "I know—you—won't want to—come back—with me. Not when you—have the chance to—live in Faerie. But if you stay here, you'll—you'll forget all about me!"

Izzy lay her cheek against Hen's hair. Somehow, through all the washings and travels and the plunge into the Liadan River, her sister still faintly smelled like a mixture of crayon wax and strawberry shampoo.

And home.

Izzy shut her eyes. She saw her parents, sitting together on the couch in the den, doing the crossword puzzle from the paper. She could almost smell her mom's perfume and feel her dad's scratchy cheek against her own. Izzy thought about the crumpled quilt on her bed, the nubby living room rug under her bare toes, her mom's overcooked broccoli. Normal, familiar, ordinary. All the things she had wanted to get away from now pulled her home like a current.

Behind them, the doors of the parlor clicked open. Selden tottered out into the hallway, followed by the other Changelings, Tom, and Marian. Dublin trotted past them and sat down at Izzy's feet.

Selden's eyes went to Hen, then Izzy. "Everything all right?"

"Everything's fine." Izzy took a deep breath. "I think I've decided to go back home with Hen."

Hen sucked the snot back up into her nostrils. "Wait, what?"

All the Changelings murmured and whispered among themselves.

"But you can't leave us, not now," said Lug. "I know! Hen could stay here with you. I'll make her a pallet right beside yours."

Hen shook her head. "I want to see my mom and dad."

Selden hobbled closer. "Izzy, are you really sure? You're one of us. You belong in Faerie just as much as on Earth."

Dree poked him in the back with her finger. "She's got a family to go back to, beetle brain."

"I know that," said Selden. He glanced over his shoulder at the Changelings standing behind him. "But there's more than one kind of family, isn't there?"

A voice behind them said, "Selden's right—you need to be sure." They turned to see Good Peter standing in the hall, dressed in a smart new suit and twirling his flute in one hand. "It isn't like the old times when you could come and go whenever you liked. Once you leave, it might be a long time before you return."

Everyone was watching Izzy, waiting for her answer. She imagined how wonderful it would be to live with the Changelings in the castle, hearing new, wonderful stories and learning how to Change. She would never have this many friends again in her life.

She shut her eyes and shook her head. "I want to stay, I really do. It's hard to explain, but my heart is telling me to go home. I wish more than anything that I didn't have to say good-bye." She slipped her hand into Hen's. "But either way, I'd be saying it to someone."

Lug's face was soaked with tears. "We don't want to say good-bye either!" he blubbered. He put one hand on Izzy's shoulder and the other on Selden's. "But we understand. Everyone has to follow their heart. Don't they, Selden?"

Selden looked down at the floor, then nodded reluctantly.

Peter's polished boots clicked against the floor as he sauntered toward them. "If we're all done with this tearful episode, then it's time we go out to the balcony. It's very rude to keep so many people waiting."

"Who's waiting on us?" asked Hen.

"Oh, no one very important," said Peter. "Only the entire citizenry of Avhalon and all the surrounding villages. They've all come to witness the return of the Changelings and the little girls who defeated the all-powerful Morvanna. There are several thousands of them crammed into the streets below."

The Changelings whispered excitedly to each other.

Izzy tilted her face to catch Selden's downturned eyes. "Let's go see them. You wouldn't want to be rude, right?"

Selden looked up and grinned. "Never."

Peter led them down the hallway to a pair of large double doors. The moment he threw them open, a deafening cheer rose up from the streets below. Izzy felt like her whole body lifted off the ground with the crescendo of the crowd. She ran with the others across the balcony to the railing and looked down. Peter had underestimated the count by half. Fairies of every type thronged the streets, leaning out of buildings and shouting up at the balcony. Lug picked Hen up and set her on his shoulders. They both raised their arms in the air and let out joyous whoops. The crowd exploded in raucous response.

Izzy joined all the others in smiling and waving down at the fairies below while the applause went on and on.

After a little while, Selden tapped her elbow. He smiled at her and mouthed the words, *Can you believe all this?*

No, she couldn't. But she let the happiness wash over her just the same.

BACK THROUGH
THE EDGEWOOD

ON A BRIGHT MORNING, after two solid days of feasting, parties, and dances celebrating Morvanna's downfall, Izzy and Hen were finally heading home. The smell of ripe apples drifted over from the orchards, where hundreds of elves were packing the fruits into sawdust-filled barrels and pressing the rest into cider. As the girls walked across the Liadan Bridge with Dublin and Peter, Izzy ran her fingers over her ears. Their tips were finally round again, thanks to a long tutorial from Dree. The rest of her felt almost back to normal too, now that she'd had a few days to let everything sink in.

Peter had agreed to take them back home on the condition that Izzy promise not to use her Changeling powers on Earth. That meant she would go back to being plain old Izzy Doyle of Everton, USA. Izzy knew she'd made the right decision to go back with Hen, but it didn't make parting with her friends any easier.

They had just finished saying good-bye to Tom and Lug

and the other Changelings. Izzy's eyes still felt puffy, and her ribs ached from Lug's hugs. She probably had enough of his hair stuck to her jacket to make a mini replica of him. Izzy looked out at the sunlight dancing over the Liadan River and tried not to think about how much she was going to miss him.

Marian had decided to stay behind. She now had seventeen adopted grandchildren to chide and fuss over. She had given Izzy a warm hug, her house key, and some instructions: "Just because I'm not going back to Everton doesn't mean I want possums destroying my house. The garden'll grow wild, and people will talk, but then again, they always did."

Izzy squeezed the key in her pocket. The cashier at the Jiggly Goat was probably still trying to convince anyone who'd listen that Marian Malloy was a witch. Izzy smiled to herself, imagining what he'd say if she ever told him the real story.

Beside her, Hen and Peter walked hand in hand. "When you take us home, be sure to leave a big sign in the woods so we can find our way back again, OK?" said Hen.

Peter tipped his nose up. "We are talking about a *fairy path*, not a truck stop. Signs won't do you any good. The paths are so hidden that finding them takes a well-trained eye—or a bit of magic." He tapped his flute against his sleeve.

"But I want to come back here!" said Hen.

"Maybe Peter will find us and bring us back soon," said Izzy, looking up at him out of the corner of her eye. "It's not like he doesn't know exactly where we live."

Peter smiled to himself but didn't say anything. Izzy had learned more about him over the past few days. It was true that he had been protecting the Changelings all along. He was forbidden to use his powers to harm a human, so he had pretended to be loyal to Morvanna while he tried to figure out a way to defeat her. On Mount Mooring, he had saved their lives when he felled the fir tree that blocked the witch's fireball. And he was the one who convinced her to use Lacrimo instead of harvesting the Changelings' hearts right away. By feeding Morvanna's insecurities and warning her to conserve her resources, he had managed to keep them all alive.

Even after learning all this, Peter was still a mystery. He'd been avoiding Izzy for the past few days, always making some excuse whenever she asked him any questions. And she had a lot: Why did he take her to Earth when she was just a baby? Who had asked him to hide her? Who were her real parents? But the only answer she could ever get out of him was a yawn and a smile.

Dublin began barking and raced down to the end of the bridge where Selden and Dree stood holding the ponies the girls would ride on their journey back to the Edgewood. At the sight of her friends, Izzy felt a sharp pang of regret. She did want to come back and see them and not have to wait for Peter.

Selden was now off his crutches, his sling hanging unused at his side. He shook his head, looking at her like she'd just volunteered for a stint in a mental institution. "I still can't believe you're leaving. And you'll be going back to school! If I didn't know better, I'd say you were a human through and through." He waved her closer. "Listen, can I tell you something?"

She leaned in toward to him.

"I know you told Peter you wouldn't do any Changing back on Earth, but—" He tapped his finger on top of her head. "You might want to stretch up just an inch or two. You know, so no one mistakes you for a baby elf."

Izzy laughed and shoved his shoulder. "Very funny. Well, what about you? What are you going to do now that everything's over?"

"Oh, there's loads to do," he said with a very official air. "First off, we've got to make sure the goblins and Unglers went all the way back to the Norlorns. No one wants them anywhere near here. Then Tom and Marian are going to start up some sort of council to govern in Avhalon."

"Are you going to be on the council?"

"And sit in meetings all day, waiting for my turn to say something? Ha! I'd rather go to school."

Selden's eyes twinkled in their mischievous way, and Izzy knew that within a week, he'd be getting into all sorts of wonderful trouble. She never thought she'd say it, but she was going to miss him.

As if he read her mind, he blushed and looked away. "Well, it's been, you know, not too terrible traveling around with you. I mean, it wasn't as bad as I thought it'd be. So…I'll see you around, I guess." He ruffled Hen's hair and patted Dublin on the head, then shoved his hands in his pockets and took off whistling down the bridge back to Avhalon.

Dree shook her head at him as she watched him go. "He's rotten at good-byes," she said. She turned to Izzy. "Listen, I hope you don't hold all that spy stuff against me. You just never can be too careful, you know."

"Totally forgot all about it," said Izzy with a smile.

Dree smiled back, then gave both the girls long, tight hugs. She slipped something wrapped in a handkerchief into Izzy's hand, then spun on her heel and took off running after Selden. With the bright sunlight streaming through her, she looked like a shimmering mirage.

Izzy unfolded the handkerchief to find a small jar of something dark and gooey. The label on the lid read, *Pollening Honey*. A scrap of paper tucked under the jar bore a message with the E's turned the wrong way:

DO NOT FORGIT US.—SƎLDƎN.

Behind her, Peter held his horse by the reins. "Are we done here, or would you like to say good-bye to every chunk of mortar on this bridge?"

Izzy took one last look at the disappearing silhouettes of her friends, then turned to face the City Road. Far in the distance, she could just make out the deep-green shade of the Edgewood.

"OK, I'm ready," she said, taking Hen's hand. "Let's go home."

ACKNOWLEDGMENTS

This story owes its existence to so many wonderful people. Thank you to my editor, Steve Geck, for believing in these characters from the very beginning, and to John Aardema, and the rest of the Sourcebooks team, for making this a beautiful book inside and out. Thank you, Elena Giovinazzo, for finding Izzy and Hen such a good home.

Special thanks to the Austin kid lit community and the excellent writers I am lucky enough to have as readers and as friends: Margo Rabb, Brad Wilson, Nikki Loftin, Samantha Clark, and Benjamin Polansky.

At its heart this book is about family. My own family is there on nearly every page. I give thanks to the many Pates, the big ones and the wee ones, the Gillespies, a York, the Soontornvats, and the Westmorelands, for inspiring the story and for keeping me going. Thank you, Mom, for passing your writing gene down to me. Thank you, Elowyn and Aven, for always asking me to tell you a tale. Please keep asking.

Most of all I want to thank my husband, the real Tom Diffley. He isn't afraid of ghosts, but he is a brilliant inventor. And I could never have finished this book without his tremendous love and support.

ABOUT THE AUTHOR

Christina Soontornvat spent her childhood in small Texas towns, eagerly waiting for the fairies to come and kidnap her. They never came, but she still believes magic things can happen to ordinary people. When not writing, Christina hangs out in science museums and takes care of her own little goblins—*ahem*—children. She lives in Austin, Texas. *The Changelings* is her first novel.